BY THE SAME AUTHOR

The Dancing Kettle
The Magic Listening Cap
Takao and Grandfather's Sword
The Promised Year
Mik and the Prowler
New Friends for Susan
The Full Circle
Makoto, the Smallest Boy
Rokubei and the Thousand Rice Bowls
The Forever Christmas Tree
Sumi's Prize
Sumi's Special Happening
Sumi and the Goat and the Tokyo Express
The Sea of Gold
In-Between Miya
Hisako's Mysteries
Journey to Topaz
Samurai of Gold Hill
The Birthday Visitor
The Rooster Who Understood Japanese

Journey Home
A Jar of Dreams
The Best Bad Thing

(Margaret K. McElderry Books)

THE HAPPIEST ENDING

THE HAPPIEST ENDING

Yoshiko Uchida

A Margaret K. McElderry Book

Atheneum 1985 New York

For Grace and Loy

Library of Congress Cataloging in Publication Data

Uchida, Yoshiko.
The happiest ending.
"A Margaret K. McElderry book."
Summary: When twelve-year-old Rinko learns that a neighbor's daughter is coming from Japan to marry a stranger twice her age, she sets out to change this arrangement and gains new insights into love and adult problems.
1. Children's stories, American. [1. Japanese Americans—Fiction. 2. Family life—Fiction] I. Title.
PZ7.U25Hap 1985 [Fic] 85-6245
ISBN 0-689-50326-1

Published simultaneously in Canada by Collier Macmillan Canada, Inc.
Composition by Maryland Linotype Composition Company, Inc.
Baltimore, Maryland
Manufactured by Fairfield Graphics
Fairfield, Pennsylvania
First Edition

THE HAPPIEST ENDING

I

HOW DID I EVER LET MAMA TALK ME INTO THIS, I wondered. How could I have been so stupid?

Here I had a nice free Saturday afternoon with no school to worry about, I'd finished my chores and helped Mama do the wash in the home laundry she runs in our basement. After that, if I'd had any brains at all, I would have been going to the five and ten to browse around or start shopping for Christmas presents.

But no, dumb me. I was rattling down to Oakland on the #3 streetcar because of an agreement I'd made with Mama. I was going for my first private Japanese-language lesson with Mama's friend, Mrs. Sugino, whom I didn't even know and whom I already didn't like.

The reason I got into this terrible predicament was because the school nurse told Mama last year that I was too skinny and looked anemic. She thought I shouldn't have to go learn Japanese every day after regular school because I had enough homework to do for my sixth-grade class.

Of course, I was absolutely ecstatic when Mama listened to the nurse, because I hate going to Japanese Language School.

"It makes me feel like a foreigner," I told Mama, "and I'm not!"

It's bad enough that I have this Japanese face, with stick-straight black hair and eyes that aren't even as pretty as my big brother Cal's. And having a name like Rinko Tsujimura, which my teachers can't pronounce, (instead of a nice simple one like Mary Smith) is another burden I have to put up with.

But Mama doesn't seem to understand. She insists my two brothers and I learn Japanese because she says it's part of our heritage.

"You're Japanese as well as American, you know," she always says. "Someday you'll be glad you learned how to read and write Japanese."

Deep down, I know she's right, and I know I should be more proud of being Japanese.

But just the same, I answer, "No, I won't. I just want to be like any other American."

But Mama goes on and on, giving me a dozen other reasons why I should study Japanese, and then I just tune her out, as I often do.

All last year I'd gloated over my kid brother, Joji (aged ten and a half), who of course had to keep on studying Japanese every day after school, since he is so plump and healthy.

"It ain't fair," he'd complained to Mama.

But she'd just told him, "Be glad you're strong and

healthy, Joji," and she warned him to stop playing hooky, which he did whenever he had the chance.

"Tough luck, kiddo," I'd say to him when I saw him gather up his books and go off to learn Japanese. "I'm *really* sorry for you," I'd say, sitting at the kitchen table munching on leftover toast covered with butter and strawberry jam. I usually grinned when I said this, looking about as sorry as a dog that just found a nice bone.

"Aw, go soak your head, Rink," Joji would say, scowling.

But today the shoe was on the other foot. It was Joji's turn to gloat.

"Have a *wonderful* time studying all afternoon," he yelled, as he banged out the back door with a football under his arm.

"Thanks, Joji, I will," I said, trying to sound lofty. And I used one of the new words I'd just learned even though I knew he wouldn't understand it.

"I know it's going to be an *edifying* experience," I yelled at him.

But what I really thought was, edifying, my foot! The only reason I was going was because Mama had given me an ultimatum.

"Either you have Mrs. Sugino tutor you, Rinko, or you start over again with the third and fourth-graders when you go back to Japanese Language School next spring."

What could I do with a choice like that? I chose Mrs. Sugino, of course.

I slouched down on the streetcar seat and was so busy

feeling sorry for myself I missed the 7th Street stop where I was supposed to get off and had to walk back two long blocks.

Mrs. Sugino lived just on the edge of Oakland's Chinatown, and I poked along past dingy little grocery stores with crates of mustard greens and long white radishes and onions spilling out onto the sidewalk. I passed the shop that sold roast duck and slabs of barbecued pork and tried not to look at the skinned rabbits hanging upside down in the window. They looked so pathetic, I couldn't stand the thought of anybody eating them. I even have trouble eating the chickens we raise in our backyard, especially since I am the one who has to feed them and collect their eggs. I feel like such a traitor, when they've been trusting us and laying eggs for us every day.

When I finally got to Mrs. Sugino's house, I saw that it was an old two-storied Victorian one, and I wondered if she had a big family to fill all the rooms upstairs. Mama hadn't told me much about her. Only that she was an excellent teacher who taught Japanese at the Buddhist Church. Mama also informed me that Mrs. Sugino was taking me on as a private pupil only as a special favor. I was prepared not to like her at all.

Gloom and doom, I thought as I rang the doorbell. And I tried hard to think of a way to get out of coming again next Saturday.

When the door opened there was a little boy staring at me, holding a half-eaten piece of bread smeared with jelly.

"Whachew want?" he asked, licking all the jelly off his bread.

He was small but solid, (like a miniature *sumo* wrestler), with hair clipped close to his skull and narrow eyes that stared at me. I noticed he had his right shoe on his left foot and vice versa, so his feet looked like they were trying to walk away from each other.

"I'm here to see your mama," I said, and squeezed my way inside before he could slam the door in my face. I went into the parlor, and he followed right behind me.

"Go call your mama," I said, and sat down on the sofa, which was about the only place there was any space to sit. The room was so jammed with furniture and knickknacks and cartons and plants and books and magazines, it looked more like somebody's attic than a parlor.

The little boy just stood there, inspecting me like a new specimen in his bug collection, so I decided I'd better get friendly.

"What's your name?" I asked, figuring that was a good place to start.

"Everybody calls me Boku."

I knew enough Japanese to know that's what little boys call themselves. "That's the word for *me*, isn't it?"

"Yup," he nodded. "I'm me."

Then he suddenly threw the rest of his sticky bread on my lap and went racing out the room yelling for his mama.

Good grief, I thought. Not only was I going to have to

study Japanese every Saturday afternoon, I was going to have to put up with that little monster as well.

I looked around the cluttered room while I waited for Mrs. S. (which is what I began calling her in my head), and knew right away that she was a saver.

Mama is a saver too. She saves everything, from old string and paper bags to empty jars and cardboard cartons. She's also saved every picture I have ever drawn since the age of two.

About the strings and jars, she says, "You never know when you're going to need them." And about my old drawings, she says, "You certainly don't expect me to throw those away in the garbage can, do you?" She also keeps every Valentine and birthday card that my two brothers and I have ever given her. She has two cartons full. But at least she keeps everything in our basement and not in the parlor, thank goodness.

I got up to look at a table piled with old copies of the *National Geographic* and saw that some were even dated back to 1930, which meant they'd been sitting there for six years. There were lots of magazines from Japan too, but of course I couldn't read those.

It wasn't the magazines I was interested in though, it was the tablecloth under them. It was made out of dozens and dozens of old cards—Christmas cards and birthday cards, and even some wedding invitations and picture post cards. They were all crocheted together with double strands of pink embroidery thread, and I thought it was just about the most fascinating tablecloth I'd ever seen. If Mama had something like that on our dining room table, I thought, Joji and I would at least have something interesting to look at during Sunday dinners when the adult conversation gets boring.

Mama likes to crochet too, but so far she hasn't thought of crocheting all her cards together. In fact, she doesn't embroider or crochet at all any more because her hands are too rough and chapped from all the washing she has to do. She says the silk threads catch on her hands now, and she can't do the kind of handiwork she did before Papa's bills got too high and she started our home laundry to help him out.

I was twisting my head and trying to read the greetings on one of the birthday cards. "May your days be filled with . . ." Then I heard a rustle behind me, and someone said, "Ah, so you're Mrs. Tsujimura's daughter."

I turned around and there was Mrs. Sugino. She turned out to be a total surprise.

II

SINCE I WAS PLANNING TO DISLIKE HER, I WAS EX-pecting Mrs. S. to be plain or ugly or even mean-looking. But she wasn't any of those things. She looked about the same age as Mama, who is thirty-eight, and I was surprised at how pretty she was. She had a thin friendly face and hair that was pulled back into a bun like Mama's, only there were little curls that escaped around her forehead.

She was wearing an apron over a long-sleeved pongee blouse with a row of tiny mother-of-pearl buttons that came right up to her throat. I thought it might have been her Sunday blouse once, but now it looked sort of tired and faded.

"Yes, I'm Rinko," I said. And I handed her the jar of pickled long radishes that Mama had sent over to her. Mama can never go see anybody without taking something, and she makes me do the same. (Of course I'd made sure the lid was screwed on good and tight so nobody would smell it on the streetcar.) I also gave her Boku's hunk of sticky bread because I didn't know what to do with it.

She thanked me for both and then said, "I see you've already met Boku. That's not his real name, of course. It's Kanzaburo, but that's too much name for a little boy, don't you think?"

Before I could answer, she asked me how old I was. When I told her, she said, "Well, how do you like being twelve and a half?" She made it sound like a place and was asking me how I liked being there.

"It's OK, but I'd rather be fifteen," I said, "or even sixteen would be nice. My big brother, Cal, is always telling me to grow up, but since he's already a sophomore in college, I'll never catch up with him."

Mrs. S. patted me on the shoulder. "Well, never mind, Rinko," she said. "Before you know it you will be twenty-three and then thirty-three and wishing you were twelve again."

I knew I wouldn't, but I didn't have a chance to tell her because she was leading the way to her kitchen. It was much bigger than ours with a black pot-bellied stove at one end and a long table covered with yellow oilcloth in the middle.

"This is where we have all our meals," she explained, and Boku immediately told me who sat at each place.

"Mr. Kinjo sits here, Papa sits here, Mr. Higa here, Johnny Ochi here, Mama here, and me here."

"We have three boarders," Mrs. S. explained, "since

we have so much room and we . . ." She stopped suddenly, as though she'd decided not to say something that had almost slipped out.

Then she took off her apron to show that she'd stopped being Boku's mama and was about to become my teacher. She had several Japanese text books on the table, and I saw that they were readers for grades three, four, and five.

I got a sick feeling in my stomach just looking at those readers with their gray covers and Japanese writing. I'd gotten up to the fifth grade reader once, but now I'd forgotten everything. It was as though I'd pulled out a stopper inside my head and all the Japanese words I'd learned had gone flowing right out. I didn't think there was even one left inside my head.

"Which book do you think you can read, Rinko?" Mrs. S. asked.

"Well . . . I guess maybe I'd better start with grade three."

"Grade three!" Boku exploded, settling into the chair next to me. "I can read Book Three and I'm only barely six!"

If his mama hadn't been sitting right there, I probably would have told him to go soak his head. Fortunately, Mrs. S. knew exactly how to deal with her smart-aleck son.

"Run out and get some wood for the stove, will you, Boku?" she asked. "It's getting a little chilly."

Boku looked out the window and didn't budge. "It's raining," he said. "I'll get wet."

Mrs. S. and I both looked out the window and sure enough it had begun to rain.

But Mrs. S. gave Boku a little nudge and said, "It's only polite rain, Boku. You'll hardly get wet at all. Go on now."

"Polite rain?" I asked.

"Yes, you know, it's not blowing or splashing. It's just coming down soft and gentle—politely."

"Oh."

I found myself smiling at Mrs. S. She smiled back, and I noticed she had a dimple in her right cheek.

"Well then, Rinko, let's start with Book Three. Now if you'll just begin here, I'll . . ."

"Mama! Help!"

It was Boku bellowing like a bull, as he dropped the wood he was carrying. We both heard it racketing down the back steps.

"Oh dear." Mrs. S. sighed. "He can be such a bother sometimes." Then she added as an afterthought, "But he *is* a good boy."

I wanted to ask her why she had only one little boy, but I know you aren't supposed to ask questions like that or ask some people why they don't have any children at all. Mama says things like that are none of my business.

I watched Mrs. S. pull on a heavy white sweater and hurry out the back door. She hadn't been gone a minute when I heard her cry out, and then there was a bumping thud.

Good grief, I thought. Now what?

I rushed to the back door and when I looked out, I saw Mrs. S. lying in a heap at the foot of the steps. Her hair had come undone and was hanging loose because all her big hairpins had fallen out. The rain had stopped being polite, and she was getting soaked.

"Oh, my gosh!" I yelled. "Are you all right, Mrs. Sugino?"

"I'm not sure," she said in a weak voice. "I slipped on the wet steps. I . . . oh . . ." She cried out again. "I think I may have broken my wrist."

Boku and I helped her get up, and she leaned on me to go back up the steps and into the house. I could tell she was in a lot of pain, but she just gritted her teeth and didn't complain.

"I'll call Papa," I said.

But Mrs. S. shook her head. "No, I'm afraid this is something your papa can't fix, even in his repair shop. Do you think you could call Dr. Kita for me?"

Boku ran to the phone in the hall and came back waving a small black book. "Here, the doctor's in here," he said.

I was so flustered, I kept looking under *D* for doctor, until Mrs. S. told me to try looking under the *Ks*. I was wishing Papa or Mama or Cal or somebody was there to help me when I heard a truck pull into the driveway.

Then a man wearing old gardening clothes came in the back door. He wasn't too tall—about like Papa—and I thought probably about his age too. He was heavy-set and solid-looking, with a wide nose and thick lips. He wore horn-rimmed glasses and had a lot of thick black hair that was combed straight back and was wet from the rain.

The minute I saw him I thought of him as a St. Bernard—solid and helpful, but not at all handsome. This is something I like to do whenever I meet somebody new. I try to think what kind of animal that person would be. I'd already decided that if Mrs. S. were a bird, she'd probably be a sparrow—friendly and cheerful. Or maybe even a hummingbird—dainty and quite beautiful.

"Oh, Mr. Kinjo. I'm so glad to see you," she said.

He took one look at her wrist, which was swelling up like a balloon, and knew exactly what to do.

"Come with me," he said, taking her good arm. "I'm taking you to see Dr. Kita."

Then he turned to me and said, "Rinko, can you stay here and look after Boku? And you'd better call your mama and tell her you'll be late."

"Sure," I answered.

Then they were gone, and Boku and I sat at the kitchen table looking at each other. He jiggled a loose front tooth with his tongue and said, "Pretty soon I ain't gonna have no teeth left in my whole mouth."

But I wasn't listening because I was thinking about something very strange.

"Say," I said. "How come Mr. Kinjo knew who I was when I've never laid eyes on him before?"

Boku sat with his elbows on the table and his chin

propped in his hands. He looked up at the ceiling and said, "I dunno. Why donchew ask him?"

"You know something," I said. "That's exactly what I'm going to do."

I could hardly wait for Mrs. S. and Mr. Kinjo to get back.

WHEN I CALLED HOME, MAMA TOLD ME OF COURSE I should stay and help Mrs. Sugino. "Help her make supper for her boarders, Rinko," Mama said. "And just stay there until Papa comes for you."

"OK, Mama," I said.

I could just see the wheels beginning to turn in her head. She would probably go straight to the kitchen and bake a sponge cake for Mrs. S. because that is what she does for anybody who is in need of comfort and love.

If I'd still had summer vacation, she probably would have told me to stay over at Mrs. Sugino's and help her until her wrist healed. That's what I did in August. Not stay with Mrs. S., of course, but with Mama's widowed friend, Mrs. Hata, who needed help harvesting her cucumbers out in East Oakland.

I'd grumbled and complained and done everything I could to get out of going, but it turned out to be just about the best month of my entire life. And now Mrs. Hata (I call her Auntie Hata), is one of my most favorite people in the world. I even like her two boys, Zenny and Abu, who turned out to be pretty good kids after I got to know them.

I was hoping Boku would turn out as well, but I thought probably no such luck. When I got back to the kitchen, I found him crunching on one of Mama's smelly yellow pickles. He'd spilled some of the juice from the jar on the table, and the whole room smelled awful.

"Hey," I said. "That was supposed to be for your mama."

He looked at me with a wicked grin. "I know it," he said.

I had a feeling then that I might be in for a lot of trouble if I didn't turn him into a friend. So I asked him what the rest of the house was like. His face lit up immediately.

"I'll show you upstairs," he said, and he shoved his half-eaten pickle back in the jar.

He kept looking back to see if I was following and led the way up the narrow staircase to the dark hallway. It smelled sort of damp and musty upstairs, and I saw that all the doors were closed. I also saw a basin standing in the hallway.

"That's a funny place for a wash basin," I remarked.

"Well, where they gonna wash their faces then?" Boku asked.

"Don't you have a bathroom?"

"Sure, downstairs. We take turns in it."

"You mean you and your mama and papa and all the boarders?"

Boku didn't bother to answer, because now he'd opened one of the doors and was peering inside. It didn't seem right to be snooping around in the boarders' rooms, but I was too curious not to look.

Inside the room I saw a narrow bed with a pair of Japanese straw slippers placed neatly beside it. There was an old brown bureau with a comb and brush sitting on top and two faded photos of a woman and a girl, both wearing kimonos, stuck in the corner of the mirror. There was also one straight-backed chair with a cushion whose stuffing was coming out. The window shade was pulled down, and the whole room looked so dark and dismal, I got the shivers just looking at it.

"Who lives here anyway?" I asked. Whoever it was must be a pretty sad and gloomy person, I thought.

"Mr. Higa," Boku answered, and in the same breath he said, "I'm not supposed to come upstairs."

"Fine time to tell me!" I exploded.

I grabbed his hand and hurried him down the stairs. Just in time, because I heard water running in the kitchen.

"Mrs. Sugino?" I called. "Did the doctor fix your wrist?"

But it wasn't Mrs. S. at all. It was a young Japanese man in a heavy navy blue sweater, standing at the sink getting a drink of water. He was leaning over it and sticking his head under the faucet without bothering to get a glass, just like my brother Cal does. I guessed he was one of the boarders.

"Hi, Johnny!" Boku shouted. "Mama's broke all her bones."

The man whirled around. "She did what?" Then seeing me, he asked, "Who are you, and what's happened to Mrs. Sugino?"

I told him as fast as I could, but I had to start at the beginning. So I told him why I had to come have private Japanese lessons from Mrs. S. in the first place, and before I knew it, I'd practically told him the entire story of my life. He just stood there listening patiently, and when I finally stopped talking, he said he knew Cal.

"My big brother? Honest?"

That's when I found out that Johnny—John Junichi Ochi—was from Tokyo and was studying at the university to be an engineer too, just like Cal. Except he said he hadn't decided yet whether to stay in America or go back to Japan after he graduated.

"Oh, you should definitely stay here," I said, although he hadn't asked for my opinion.

He didn't seem exactly thrilled at my suggestion. He just shrugged and said, "Well, it depends on a lot of things." I thought he was going to say the same thing Cal often does, which is, "Who's going to hire a Japanese engineer?" But instead he said, "You know, what I'd really like to do is become an actor, like Sadakichi Hartmann."

"Like who?"

Johnny told me about this actor with a Japanese

mother and a German father who also wrote books and poetry. "I'd like to do all those things too," he said.

What a dream, I thought. I'd never in my life met anybody who wanted to be an actor or a poet or a writer, and here was Johnny Ochi wanting to be all three.

Now that he'd mentioned it, I thought he'd be wonderful in the movies. He was really handsome, with dreamy eyes, dark eyebrows and a tall thin nose. Instead of thinking of what animal he reminded me of, I immediately thought of him as a prince. In fact, he looked like a Japanese Tyrone Power, and I knew if my best friend, Tami, saw him, she would want to marry him immediately. Of course she is only my age, but she is always looking out for what her mother calls "a good prospect." Her mother is, in fact, the busiest matchmaker in our church.

I think Johnny wanted to talk more about becoming an actor and a poet, but at that very instant Boku began yelling, "Mama's back! Mama's back!"

And sure enough, Mrs. S. came in with her right arm in a big white cast. Mr. Kinjo was right behind her, carrying her purse for her.

"My wrist is broken, all right," she said, as though it was just one of those things fate had planned for her.

"Well, don't worry," I said. "Mama told me to stay and help you get supper. I'm pretty good at cooking rice."

"That's what Mrs. Hata told me," Mr. Kinjo said, as he helped Mrs. S. off with her coat. "She said you were a great help to her this summer."

He'd done it again! He acted as though he knew everything about me, and it gave me the willies. So I looked him straight in the eye (which I can't seem to do when I'm talking to a white person—especially a grownup), and I just flat out asked him, "Say, how come you know all about me when I don't even know you?"

Mr. Kinjo chuckled as though I'd just told him a funny joke and explained how he'd met Auntie Hata after she started working as the housekeeper for the bachelors in the dormitory behind our Japanese church.

"Everybody in the dormitory knows about you, Rinko," he went on. "Mrs. Hata talks as much about you as she does about her two boys. She calls you her 'summer daughter'."

"She does?"

I liked the sound of that. I guessed she called me that so people wouldn't get me mixed up with her *real* and *permanent* daughter, Teru, who'd been raised by her grandparents in Japan. In fact, Auntie Hata hadn't even seen her for eighteen years. I almost said all that to Mr. Kinjo, but it was too long a story. Besides, I had to help Mrs. S., who was trying to get supper started with only one good hand.

I washed the rice and put it on the stove to cook. I washed two bunches of spinach until all the sand was gone, while Mrs. S. toasted the sesame seeds to sprinkle over it. I even washed and salted six mackerel with their round glassy eyes staring at me. I would have balked if Mama had asked me to do that at home, but what could I do when somebody with an arm in a cast had asked for help? I picked the mackerel up by their tails, stuck them under the broiler and wished I wasn't going to have to eat one for supper. But Mrs. S. had already asked me to stay.

"You can sit at my husband's place," she said to me. "He's so busy now that he's started selling insurance, he won't be home for dinner."

"Again?" Boku whined. "Papa's never home!"

"I know." Mrs. S. sighed, and she made a face, which I guess was meant for Mr. Sugino even though he wasn't there to see it. I got the funny feeling that even if he was her husband, she didn't like him very much.

"Well, what am I going to do?" she asked no one in particular.

I certainly didn't know.

But now that the smells of supper had begun to drift through the house, everybody gathered in the kitchen. And that was when the third boarder, Mr. Higa, who lived in the dark gloomy room upstairs, finally came home.

IV

"RINKO, THIS IS MR. HIGA," MRS. S. SAID TO ME.

I knew immediately that I'd been right about him. He looked just like his room—sad and lonely. He was definitely a bassett hound, I thought. He looked as though his shoes pinched, but he'd learned to put up with it.

He had close-cropped gray hair that made his head look sort of flat on top. And he was hunched over, with a tic in his right shoulder, which I learned came from working in a laundry and ironing clothes all day. That would certainly give anybody a nervous tic and make them look sad.

I help Mama iron the flat things, like sheets and pillow cases and handkerchiefs, but it's not much fun, and I would certainly hate to spend the rest of my life looking at damp, rumpled clothes and doing nothing but iron all day. What's there to hope for in a life like that?

Papa says everybody needs to have hope and a dream. But poor Mr. Higa didn't seem to have either one, and I immediately began to think of him as Mr. Sad Higa.

Nobody said grace before dinner like we do at home, and Boku was already chewing on a mouthful of rice and fish when Mr. Kinjo suddenly produced a bottle of saké and some tiny wine cups.

"I want all of you to celebrate something with me tonight," he said with a huge smile.

"What is it?" Mr. Sad Higa asked, looking startled. "Have we forgotten your birthday?"

"No, no, it is something even more wonderful than a birthday, and I can keep it a secret no longer," Mr. Kinjo began. "Today Mrs. Hata and I set the date for the wedding."

"Why, Mr. Kinjo, how wonderful!" Mrs. S. said, and she got so excited she spilled all the rice she'd picked up so carefully with the chopsticks in her left hand.

Johnny Ochi jumped up from his seat and went over to slap Mr. Kinjo on the back and shake his hand. Even Mr. Sad Higa was smiling as he held up his wine cup to be filled. Everybody was talking at once and congratulating Mr. Kinjo. Everybody, that is, except me.

What I said was, "Mrs. Hata? You mean *my* Auntie Hata?"

How could my wonderful Auntie Hata get married again? Her husband hadn't even been dead a year, and I knew for a fact that his spirit still hovered around in her house. We'd both heard him one night, and he had even sent Auntie Hata a vital message through me.

It seemed downright disloyal for Auntie Hata to be marrying somebody else so soon. Besides, I thought, what would happen when she died? Wouldn't she be buried next to Mr. Hata? Then what would happen to the second husband when *he* died? Would he be buried on the other side of Auntie Hata, so she'd be lying with a husband on each side like a filling in the middle of a sandwich?

"For heaven's sake," I said out loud. "You can't marry Auntie Hata!"

Mr. Kinjo threw back his head and laughed so hard I could see all the gold fillings in his back teeth.

"My dear Rinko," he said. "It's *not* your Auntie Hata I'm going to marry. It's her daughter, Teru. I've sent her the boat fare so she can come from Japan in December. Then I will have a wife, and Mrs. Hata will have her daughter with her once more, and everyone will be happy."

He beamed, and I knew he was waiting for me to say how wonderful that was. But instead, I did a terrible thing. And considering how shy I am about speaking out at school, I don't know whatever made me do it. What I did was to blurt out, "But Teru's only nineteen! You're too old for her!"

That's when everybody stopped talking. It was as though the tubes of a radio had suddenly blown out, and except for the sounds of Boku chewing with his mouth open, there was nothing but dead silence. Everybody was so embarrassed, no one could think of a thing to say, not even Mrs. S.

Mr. Kinjo just stood there holding his wine cup, his mouth half open, with no words coming out. He looked as though somebody had kicked him in the stomach. And that somebody was me.

So what I said next was, "Well, I was just telling the truth." But that only made things worse.

Mama and Papa always tell me to be truthful and honest, and I try to be most of the time. Of course sometimes I figure it's OK to bend the truth a little, just to be friendly. Like the time our teacher had her hair cut.

"How do you like it?" she'd asked me, patting the nice trimmed ends.

Personally, I didn't think it looked that great, but I knew she was waiting for me to tell her I liked it fine, so that's exactly what I did.

Papa probably would've called that being dishonest. If he likes you, he'll let you know. If he doesn't, you'd better watch out. Mama tells Papa that sometimes he is too honest.

"How can anybody be too honest?" he will ask.

Then Mama reminds him of the times he's blurted out remarks like, "My, you've gained a lot of weight," or "You certainly have gotten gray lately."

"Nobody likes to hear things like that," Mama says.

But Papa will shake his head and say, "Well, I was only telling the truth."

And that's exactly what I'd said to Mr. Kinjo. But what I should have done was to use my head and bend the truth a little bit. Now all the happiness had drained right out of his face, and he looked as though he wanted to cry.

"I realize there is a vast difference in our ages . . ." he began.

Then Mrs. S. finally recovered from the shock I'd given everybody and said, "Well, I think it's just lovely, Mr. Kinjo. Mrs. Hata must be so happy to know her daughter will be coming back to America at last. I know it's a dream she's had for a long, long time."

Then she turned to Boku and told him that many of the early Japanese immigrants had sent their children back to Japan to be raised by relatives, because they couldn't care for them while they worked in the fields and farms.

"They wanted their children to have a better life than they had here," Mrs. S. explained to Boku. "That's why Mrs. Hata sent her baby daughter, Teru, to be raised by her grandparents in Japan."

Of course Boku wasn't the least bit interested in what his mother was saying. He was too busy eating his supper. But Mrs. S. couldn't seem to stop talking. I guess she was afraid if she did, there would be that awful silence again.

Eventually Johnny found his tongue too, and he said, "Well, I say good for you, Kinjo. You've finally found yourself a bride. Congratulations! *Kampai*!" He raised his wine cup in a toast, and everybody drank to Mr. Kinjo and his new bride.

Mr. Sad Higa didn't look sad any more, and I discovered that he actually *did* have something to hope for and dream about.

"What a Christmas this will be," he said in a raspy

voice. "Kinjo's bride will come from Japan, and I have finally saved enough money to return to Japan in time for the new year."

"To be reunited with your wife and daughter after seventeen long years," Mrs. S. added, as though she were telling the happy ending to a fairy tale.

It seemed as though everybody was happy except me. I still didn't think Mrs. Hata's daughter should marry a man old enough to be her father. She hadn't even met him, and it didn't seem fair. I just knew it wasn't right, and I felt as though Mr. Hata's spirit was speaking to me again, like he'd done when I was at Auntie Hata's. He was saying it was up to me to save his daughter, Teru. And I decided right then and there that I would.

V

I THINK THAT SUPPER AT MRS. SUGINO'S WAS JUST about the longest one I have ever suffered through. It felt like it lasted three hours, and although everybody tried to be cheerful and to forget what I'd said, the smile never came back to Mr. Kinjo's face. I felt terrible about having made him feel so bad.

I knew I should apologize or say something to make him feel better, but I didn't know how. It's very hard for me to say I'm sorry to anybody. I will pick a fight with my kid brother, Joji, and even if I know I was wrong, I will never say I'm sorry to him. What I usually do is squash his beanie down over his eyes or poke him in the ribs, and he knows that's my way of making up with him. But I certainly couldn't do that to Mr. Kinjo.

What I did was to keep my eyes on my plate during most of the meal because I couldn't bear to look at anybody. Boku kept watching me and finally offered to eat my mackerel since I wasn't eating it.

"Sure, take it," I said, and slid my plate over to him.

I was never so glad to see anybody as I was to see Papa when he finally arrived. He came in the back door, still wearing the overalls he wears in his shop. And he brought a sponge cake covered with wax paper, just like I thought he would. I could smell the vanilla in it and thought it was probably still warm. But I didn't feel like having even a small piece. I knew I didn't deserve it.

Papa greeted everybody with a handshake and told Mrs. S. how sorry he was about her accident.

"Are you sure you're all right?" he asked. "We'll try to find somebody to come help you during the week, and of course Rinko can help you on Saturdays."

I saw that he and Mama had already arranged everything. I don't even remember what Mrs. S. said to all that, because I scarcely listened. I'd already carried my dishes to the sink and could hardly wait to get out of there.

I kept wishing Johnny would help me clear the rest of the table. But he didn't. So I did it by myself, stacking everything at the table even though Mama says that's not polite.

I washed the dishes as fast as I could and then grabbed Papa's arm and steered him toward the back door.

"Let's go, Papa," I urged. "Let's go."

I didn't even say good-bye to anybody, but I heard Boku yell, "Seeya next Saturday, Rinky."

I certainly hope not, I said under my breath.

All the way home I sat like a clam in the front seat next to Papa and didn't say a word.

"What's wrong, Rinko?" Papa asked.

But I couldn't tell him, and thank goodness, Papa didn't ask again. He just left me alone, like I hoped he would. And when I got home, I didn't tell Mama either, because I knew she'd say I'd been rude and thoughtless. She would probably tell me it was wonderful that Mrs. Hata could be reunited with her daughter at last, and that Mr. Kinjo was a very good man.

But I certainly couldn't keep everything inside. I was about ready to explode and just had to tell somebody who would agree with me. As soon as I answered all of Mama's questions about Mrs. S. and told her she was all right, I went into the hall. I closed the three doors that open into it and called my best friend, Tami, who insists these days that I call her Kathryn.

That is the name she picked for herself after I decided to use Evangeline as my middle name because it sounded so elegant. I discovered it when our teacher told us about the poem, *Evangeline, A Tale of Acadie*, by Henry Wadsworth Longfellow. I haven't told Tami Kathryn yet, but actually I'm not too crazy about that name anymore and am looking around for another nice *E* name so I won't have to change my initials. So far my list includes Emily, Emma, Elizabeth and Euphemia.

I told Tami Kathryn (I've decided to call her TK for short), all about Teru and Mr. Kinjo, and she let out such a screech, I had to hold the receiver away from my ear.

"You mean he's forty?" she screamed.

"At least. Maybe older. He looks older than Papa."

"And she's only nineteen? That's positively awful. What're you going to do?"

"I'd sure like to save her . . ." I began.

"From a fate worse than death," TK finished. She often interrupts me like that, and she also loves being dramatic. Sometimes I think there is a twenty-nine-year-old woman locked inside her twelve-and-a-half-year-old body.

"What can I do?" I asked.

"I don't know, but you've got to think of something," TK said, as though everything was my fault, and I was the one who had to make things right.

"Well, I'll try," I said, but I honestly didn't have the faintest idea how.

That night when I went to bed, I didn't do my stretching exercises to try to grow taller, I just lay in the darkness and thought about how I could save Teru.

What I had to do, I decided, was to contact Mr. Hata's spirit again right away. It was a good thing I had this gift of being able to communicate with the dead—not all the dead, of course. Actually, it was only Mr. Hata and just that one time when I was staying at Auntie Hata's.

I wasn't sure how to make him come to me now and whether he could find me here in Berkeley in my own bed. But I had to try. I sat up in bed and concentrated real hard.

"OK, Mr. Hata," I said. "You told me at that awful supper tonight that it was up to me to save your daughter. Now tell me how."

Nothing.

"Just a minute," I said to him in case he was on his way.

I thought I should look more like a medium if I was going to be one. Actually, I've never seen a real live medium, but I thought probably they must look like those fortune tellers I've seen pictures of, with dangling earrings and silken scarves around their heads, peering into a crystal ball.

I certainly didn't have a crystal ball, and I was too lazy to get out of bed and look for my one and only silk scarf that Cal gave me last year. So I just pulled the back of my pajama top over my head and hoped that would do for now.

"Well, Mr. Hata?" I asked. "Help me!"

More of nothing.

I reached up into the darkness with my arms and waved them around, trying to feel his presence, because I honestly do believe in the spirit world. Auntie Hata once told me that if we really believe in spirits, then they're out there for us. She said they can float through millions of miles of space, because for them there is no time or space as we know it, and they come back to help us poor creatures still locked inside our human bodies on earth.

It gave me the shivers to hear her talk like that, but I believe she's right. And it's kind of a good feeling to know we can still connect up with people even after they're dead.

I know the California Maidu Indians believed the

same thing, because I read about the big burnings they used to have. They would burn huge piles of clothing and food which went up in smoke to the spirit world as gifts to their dead relatives. I certainly hope when I'm in the spirit world, somebody will think of sending me a whole pile of nice smoky gifts too.

Maybe, I thought, what I needed to do to call back Mr. Hata's spirit was to build a spirit fire for him. Maybe . . .

Just then I heard the knob of my door turning slowly. An icy chill raced down my spine and made all my toes tingle.

"Rinko, are you still up?" a voice asked.

But it wasn't Mr. Hata's spirit at all. It was only Mama.

"No, Mama, I'm already half asleep," I answered.

"Well, settle down and get to sleep then."

I got back under the covers and lay very still, waiting. I planned on waiting until Mr. Hata gave me some kind of sign. But, unfortunately, I fell asleep, and if Mr. Hata's spirit ever did come to me that night, I never knew it.

VI

I WAITED ALL WEEK FOR SOME KIND OF MESSAGE from Mr. Hata's spirit, but I didn't get a thing. Not even a little glimmer. And then it was Saturday and time for me to go have another Japanese lesson with Mrs. S.

I wanted to go help Mrs. S. because I knew she needed me, but I certainly didn't want to see Mr. Kinjo again, not after the way I'd insulted him. And I wasn't crazy about the thought of putting up with Boku for a whole day either.

"I think I'm sick," I said to Mama. "I think my tonsils are swollen again. And my knees ache. Maybe I'm getting the flu."

But Mama, who knows absolutely everything that is going on inside my head, told me that Mrs. Sugino was counting on me. "She's got help during the week, Rinko, but she really needs you today. You know that, don't you?"

"Uh-huh. But what about my flu?"

Mama came to feel my forehead.

"You don't seem to have a fever, Rinko. Let me see your throat."

"Ahhhhh."

"Your tonsils are tucked away nicely, Rinko, and your throat looks fine."

"Well, my knees ache."

Mama gave me a hot water bottle for my knees. "Boil some water and don't forget to squeeze the air out of the bag before you put in the stopper," she said. I guess she was thinking of all the times I'd forgotten, and the hot water bottle looked more like a football. Then she started downstairs to do her wash in the basement.

"Don't you want me to help you iron this afternoon?" I called out in a last effort. But Mama was gone. She'd had enough of me.

I thought of going to talk to Papa, but I could see from the window that he was under his old Model T, working on something or other, and I knew I wouldn't get any sympathy from him.

Joji had gone on an errand to buy some baking powder and sugar for our neighbor, so I knew Cal was alone in the room they shared. I decided to try him, and I knocked on his door.

"Yeah?"

"It's me."

"What d'you want, Rink? I'm cramming for a midterm."

"I need help."

Silence.

"It's urgent, Cal!"

"Well, OK then, but just for a minute."

Cal was sprawled on his bed reading *Popular Mechanics*.

"Hey, I thought you were studying."

Cal grinned at me. "Well, it was worth a try. What's wrong?"

"Just everything," I moaned.

I flopped down on Joji's bed and poured out my whole sorry story about what had happened last Saturday at Mrs. Sugino's.

Sometimes I can do that with Cal, tell him everything on my mind, that is. Sometimes I can tell him things I can't even tell Mama or Papa or anyone else. And if Cal's in a good mood, he'll really listen and try to help.

Like the time he convinced me I shouldn't give up trying to become a schoolteacher, even though he'd almost given up on becoming an engineer. He told me I should keep on hoping and trying, like Mama and Papa wanted us to, and not ever give up.

"Who knows," he said. "By the time you're grown up, maybe they'll be hiring Japanese American teachers in the public schools."

So I'm still holding on to my dream, and I'm going to keep trying, just like Cal told me to.

Fortunately, this happened to be one of Cal's good days. He put down his magazine, locked his hands behind his head, and really listened.

When I'd finished telling him everything, I said, "So you see, I just can't go back and face Mr. Kinjo today.

And I still really do think he's too old for Teru. I've just got to think of a way to help her."

I didn't mention Mr. Hata's spirit though, because there are some things I can't tell even Cal.

Cal sat up and looked at me. "You mean *that's* your big problem?" he asked. "For pete's sake, Rink, grow up! You're probably going to say and do a lot of dumb things in your life before it's over, but you won't solve anything by running away from your problems. Besides, you learned something from your experience, didn't you?"

I tried hard to think what I'd learned. But I finally had to ask, "What?"

"That you should mind your own business—especially when it comes to someone else's marriage. Besides," Cal went on, "Mr. Kinjo is the one who sent Teru her boat fare so she could come to America, isn't he? Do you think she can just ignore that and marry somebody else? She's made a commitment to him. She can't go back on her word now. Can't you see that? Now quit being such a baby and go help Mrs. Sugino."

Cal swung his long legs off the creaky bed, grabbed his books and headed for the door. "I really have to crack the books now, Rink," he said. And he was gone.

"Thanks a heap for all your sympathy, California," I said, using his full and proper name. But he didn't hear me. He was already out the back door.

I went over to sit on his bed and looked at all the stuff he had spread out on his messy desk. There were three pictures of his new girl friend, Susie, propped up by his lamp. Two were of Susie all dressed up in her new suit, wearing short white gloves, a hat with a little veil, and real high heels. She is slim and willowy and looked really beautiful.

The other snapshot was of Susie and Cal at Muir Woods. They were standing in front of an enormous redwood tree, holding hands, with the breeze rumpling their hair. Instead of looking at the camera, they were looking at each other, and they looked as though they were really and truly in love.

Cal talks more about Susie than about any other girl friend he's had, and he's taken her to every dance of the Japanese Students Club at the university this semester. He's also gone to Petaluma to meet her parents.

I've never been to Petaluma, but I'd love to go there some day, especially in the summer when they have their "Ugly Dog Contest." I could really love a town that had a contest like that, and I wish Joji still had his bassett hound, Maxie, because I know he'd win first prize for sure.

Cal goes to Petaluma so often now, whenever he asks Papa if he can borrow the car on a Saturday, I ask, "Going to Pet-a-luma again?"

"Yup," Cal will say.

"Oh," I say, "I thought you were going to Pet-a-doggy, an ugly doggy. Ha, ha, ha."

Then Cal gives me one of his thoroughly disgusted looks and says, "Aw, grow up, Rink!" And he goes stalking off.

Maybe the reason I tease Cal is because I wish he would take me on a picnic or to the movies once in a while instead of his girl friend. But I know he never will, because I will always and forever be just his kid sister, no matter what.

If Cal did marry Susie, I thought, she would become my sister-in-law, (I've always wanted a sister) and then maybe we could all three do things together. That would suit me fine, because I like Susie a lot. I think she and my tall good-looking big brother would be exactly right for each other.

That's what a wedding is supposed to be, I thought. Two people like Cal and Susie, who are in love, getting married. Not a match like Teru and Mr. Kinjo who didn't even know each other. Who didn't fit at all. Who would look like a father and daughter when they walked down the street together.

I love and adore going to weddings, although I've only been to one, and that was when Mama and Papa were the go-between for the couple. Not that they really needed a go-between. They'd fallen in love all by themselves and managed just fine. But Mama said it was a formality for most Japanese people to have an official go-between at their weddings.

Maybe Auntie Hata would ask Mama and Papa to be the official go-between for Teru and Mr. Kinjo, I thought. Then they'd be responsible for matching Teru up with the wrong man.

The longer I sat there looking at the picture of Cal and Susie, the more I knew Cal was wrong. It *was* my business to rescue Teru, and it wasn't too late, even if she'd already made a commitment. Sometimes I think you can say you've made a mistake and need to change your mind.

"You're wrong, Cal," I said. "I'm not going to let Teru make the biggest mistake of her life. One of these days you'll see I was right, and you'll realize I *am* growing up!"

I ran to get my coat, stuck two nickels in my pocket for carfare and hurried down to the basement.

"Mama, I'm going to Oakland now," I called.

"Good, Rinko. Give Mrs. Sugino my regards."

"OK, Mama, I will."

What I didn't tell her was that I wasn't going to see Mrs. S. just yet. First I was going to stop at the church dormitory and have a talk with Auntie Hata. If the spirit of her dead husband wasn't going to give me any help, maybe she would. At least she was alive and would answer back.

I was in such a hurry to get there, I ran all the way to the corner of Grove Street and nearly went crazy waiting twenty minutes for the street car to come.

VII

I WAS HOPING I WOULDN'T RUN INTO THE MINISTER when I walked past the chapel on my way to the old wooden dormitory building in back. But that is exactly what I did. He was sweeping the steps of the parsonage, which is tacked on to the rear of the chapel.

What I think happened is that the church people suddenly thought of the minister after they'd finished building the chapel and stuck on a house for him and his family in back. The trouble is, Reverend Mitaka hasn't found a wife yet, so he's rattling around in the parsonage all by himself.

He looked so different. Not a bit like the Reverend Mitaka I see on Sundays all dressed up in his black preaching suit, looking pious. He was wearing baggy pants and an old brown sweater with a hole in the elbow, and he didn't have on his glasses. I had to look twice to make sure it really was the minister.

"Well, hello, Rinko," he said when he saw me. "What brings you here on a Saturday?"

I guess he thought I'd made a mistake and turned up a day early for Sunday School.

"I came to see Auntie Hata," I said right off, so he'd know I hadn't come to visit him.

"Oh, I see," he said.

I thought he sounded disappointed that it wasn't him I'd come to see, so I said, "Golly, you look like a regular normal person today."

Reverend Mitaka tried to stop a smile that crept over his serious face. "Well, I like to think I'm always fairly normal, Rinko."

"What I meant was, I think I like you better in those old baggy clothes sweeping the steps than preaching up there in the pulpit in your Sunday suit."

The minute the words were out of my mouth, I knew I'd done it again. I was being like Papa, saying things people don't really want to hear. So I quickly said something I knew he'd like.

"Mama thinks your sermons are truly edifying," I said. And I knew that, unlike Joji, he would understand my nice new word.

"Why, thank you, Rinko," he said.

Then since I had absolutely nothing more to say to him, I just switched off the conversation like I do my reading lamp when I'm ready to go to sleep.

"Well, so long," I said, and I ran toward the dormitory.

I thought I heard him chuckling behind me, but I didn't turn to look. I hurried up the rickety steps of the dormitory two at a time and pushed open the front door, because I knew it wouldn't be locked.

"Auntie Ha . . ." I started, when I ran smack into her arms.

"I saw you from the window," she said, giving me an enormous hug. "My, but it's good to see you."

Under her big apron, I could see Auntie Hata was wearing her usual rumpled, faded cotton dress and a heavy sweater that looked like it might have belonged once to Mr. Hata. I wondered if maybe that made her feel like he was still with her.

She felt good and warm to hug, and she smelled like strawberries. So I knew she was still using the peddler's hair pomade, probably to make her shoes shine, like she used to.

"You smell good," I said, and then I told her I couldn't stay long.

"I know," she said. "You're helping Mrs. Sugino today."

"Mama told you?"

"No, it was Mr. Kinjo. You know, one of Mrs. Sugino's boarders."

I hadn't planned on talking about him the minute I walked in, and I didn't know how to tell her what a big mistake she was making to let her daughter marry him But Auntie Hata didn't give me a chance to begin.

"You know about my Teru and Mr. Kinjo, don't

you?" she asked, with a big smile on her round rosy-cheeked face. "We're having a party here tonight to celebrate."

She quickly led me through the foyer and into the front room. It was big and barren, with nothing but a green tiled fireplace in the corner, and in the center, a long table made of wood planks resting on two saw horses. There wasn't another stick of furniture in the room except for some wooden folding chairs, and I felt glad I wasn't one of those bachelors with no family who had to live in such a dreary place.

I was surprised to see the plain old board table covered with pink crepe paper, and in the center were two Japanese folding fans spread open with some folded paper cranes around them.

"How do you like my decorations?" Auntie Hata asked. "You know, fans are for good luck. So your good fortune will spread," she explained, making half-circles with her hands like an opening fan.

"Of course my good fortune has already spread," she added. "First your mama and papa found me this nice job as housekeeper. And now my daughter will be here by Christmas. Imagine!"

I knew Auntie Hata expected me to say how wonderful that was. I tried to look happy, but my face just sort of scrunched up into a frown.

Finally I said, "Auntie Hata, aren't there any nice bachelors here at the dormitory?"

"Of course. They're all nice."

"I mean somebody . . . uh, younger. Like Teru."

Auntie Hata knew immediately what was on my mind.

"Come with me into the kitchen," she said. "I've got to chop some onions to put in with the chicken."

I guess it was easier for her to talk to me while she kept her hands busy. I never saw anybody peel onions and chop them up so fast. And all the time she was chopping, she was talking to me.

"Mr. Kinjo is a good man, Rinko," she began. "He's honest and kind and will take good care of my daughter. With him she will be safe and secure and won't have to worry about having enough to eat."

"I know, but . . ."

Auntie Hata wasn't finished. "The younger men here are still struggling just to support themselves. They can't afford a wife yet, don't you see? It's taken Mr. Kinjo a lot of years to save up so he could send for a wife."

I had a feeling Auntie Hata was going to say more so I jumped in while I had the chance.

"But Auntie Hata," I said, "I thought people got married because they fell in love. Like my brother Cal and Susie."

Auntie Hata rubbed her eyes with the back of her hand, and I wasn't sure if it was the onions or me that was making her cry.

"Ah that . . ." she said in a low voice. "Love will come later, Rinko. Like it did for so many of us who came from Japan to marry men we knew only by photographs."

She took a deep breath and went on. "Marriage isn't all love and romance, Rinko. Sometimes it's two people trying to manage . . . just keeping the children fed . . .

like Mr. Hata and me. And then, you know, a closeness comes—a sort of caring. Maybe that's love. I don't know. Maybe there're all kinds of love in this world."

Auntie Hata sniffled and wiped her nose on the corner of her apron.

"Are you really crying now, Auntie Hata?"

"Only from the onions," she said. "Listen, Rinko, I'm so happy I could shed tears of joy! Think how long it would have taken me to save up enough money to send for Teru. Maybe I never would have. I know my husband out there in the spirit world is happy for us too."

"He is? Did he come and tell you that?"

No wonder he hadn't come to help me, I thought.

Auntie Hata shook her head. "No, he didn't come tell me, but I know. I just know."

Auntie Hata looked sad now, and I knew she was wishing Mr. Hata was still alive and could be here when Teru finally came home.

I'd done it again. First to Mr. Kinjo and now to Auntie Hata. I had become a regular killjoy. Miss-too-honest-minding-other-people's-business-killjoy. That was me!

I knew it was time to leave and told Auntie Hata I had to go.

"Come again soon, Rinko," she said. And she gave me a hug to show that she still loved me in spite of what I'd said.

She came with me to the front door, still dabbing at her eyes. I was halfway down the steps when she called out after me, "It's going to be all right, Rinko. You'll see."

And that was when I knew none of them could really understand. Not Auntie Hata or Mrs. S. or Mama or Papa. Not one of them could know how Teru would feel because they weren't nineteen anymore.

So I knew I couldn't count on any of them or Mr. Hata's spirit or even Cal. That left just me and TK. But I knew it was mostly me.

VIII

THANKSGIVING WAS STILL A WEEK AWAY, BUT I could feel it coming by the smell of the leaves Papa burned in the backyard and Mama's huge white chrysanthemums blooming, and on some days, the damp smell of the ocean mists.

I'm always happy when November comes around, because then I know it's almost time for the good things, like Thanksgiving and Christmas, and I love waiting and getting ready for them.

I also love Armistice Day when we have a school assembly at 11:00 A.M. on the eleventh month to remember when the terrible world war ended in 1918. This year our class gets to sing "Over There" and "It's a Long Way to Tipperary" at the assembly, and I can hardly wait. But sometimes I get sad and shivery with goose bumps when I sing those songs and think about those poor doughboys who died fighting in Europe.

"Why do you like to sing those songs then, if they make you feel so sad?" TK asks.

But I guess it's for the same reason Papa likes to sing the songs he learned when he was a young boy in Japan.

"It's good to remember the past," he says, "even if it does make you sad. Besides," he adds, "it's a good sadness."

Papa is so patriotic, he gets out the big American flag that stays all wrapped up in tissue paper in our cupboard drawer until a special holiday like the Fourth of July or Armistice Day. Then he hangs it on our front porch and goes out in front to admire it.

He stands with a big smile on his face and says proudly, "Now isn't that a beautiful sight?"

Some years we have Armistice Day parades in town with marching bands and gray-haired veterans of the Spanish American War riding in open cars, waving and nodding.

That is another thing I love—parades! I could spend a whole day watching one, but I could never march in one myself. I often wonder how those marchers feel with everybody lined up on the sidewalk staring at them. I know I'd immediately turn into the meek and mild self I am at school and could never strut in front of a band like those baton twirlers do.

I guess the only time I could act like that would be at home when nobody is watching. And sometimes I do. I turn on the radio music real loud and dance all around the living room, but only if everybody happens to be out of the house. That is the Unseen Rinko, when I can become ANYBODY and do ANYTHING. But nobody knows that Rinko except me.

Well, anyway, several days before Thanksgiving, Mama sprang one of her suppertime announcements on us.

"You know, I've been thinking," she began.

Oh-oh, I thought, what now? That was how Mama had begun when she told us she wanted to start the home laundry. That was usually how she began when she asked me to do something I didn't want to do.

I looked at Cal and Joji, but I could tell Cal had already tuned Mama out. He was probably thinking about Susie and wishing he was with her instead of stuck with us. As for Joji, he was gobbling up Mama's stew just the way Boku eats his rice and pickles. In fact, there was quite a resemblance between the two, and it was my misfortune to be stuck with them both.

Only Papa and I stopped eating and looked at Mama.

"What now?" Papa asked.

He knew all about Mama's ideas too. Not that he doesn't get some pretty wild ones himself. Like the time he closed his barber shop and opened the garage and repair shop he'd always dreamed of having. Of course, that turned out to be one of his better ideas, because it made his life's dream come true. Papa says there are times in life when you just have to take a chance, and I guess that was about the best chance he ever took.

"I've been wondering," Mama began again, "how poor Mrs. Sugino is going to manage to cook a Thanksgiving dinner with her arm still in a cast."

I knew the doctor had said it wasn't healing properly,

and the last time I saw Mrs. S. she was quite depressed about the whole thing.

"Maybe I will spend the rest of my life being one-armed and wearing this miserable cast," she'd worried.

And I'd comforted her the way Mama comforts me, saying, "It'll be much better tomorrow, you'll see." But actually, I knew that probably didn't apply to broken bones.

"We don't have room to invite the Suginos and their boarders here," Mama went on, "so I thought it would be nice if we all went there and had a joint Thanksgiving dinner, which I could prepare in Mrs. Sugino's kitchen."

Mama looked around the table, expecting us to tell her what a lovely idea that was. But there was only total silence.

Then Cal said, "Well, I won't be here, Ma. I'm going to Petaluma to be with Susie and her folks."

Papa was rubbing his chin and giving the idea some thought. Then finally he said, "I think that would be a fine and neighborly thing to do, Mama."

I should have known. Papa almost always sides with Mama about most things unless he thinks she is being unreasonable or overly pious about what's sinful and what's not.

Mama cleared her throat and then said with a light laugh, "Well, as a matter of fact, I've already talked to Mrs. Sugino about it, and she thought it was a fine idea too. She's ordering a sixteen-pound turkey, and I'll take over the rest of the dinner."

She'd done it again! Mama had gone ahead and decided to do something all by herself and then let us think we'd helped her decide.

I wasn't at all happy about the idea myself. "Aw, Mama," I said. "I'd rather eat at home."

"It looks like everything's already settled, Rinko," Papa said. "You might as well accept it gracefully."

But graceful was the last thing I felt. I felt just like Wednesday's child in the poem that goes, "Wednesday's child is full of woe." That was me all right.

"Be a good sport, Rink," Cal urged.

Easy for him to say, I thought. He wasn't even going to be there. And even Joji, who I'd been counting on for support, let me down.

"Gosh, we ain't never had a sixteen-pound turkey before!" He beamed. "Wonder how it'll taste?"

I knew then that my goose was cooked. Or rather, I guess it was my turkey.

I really didn't want to spend my Thanksgiving with Mr. Kinjo. But I consoled myself by remembering that John Tyrone Power Ochi, the Prince, would be there. Also, I was getting very curious to see Mrs. Sugino's husband, since I still hadn't seen him, not even once. He was a mysterious presence who caused Mrs. S. to make faces at him when he wasn't there. Sometimes I wondered if she even liked him at all.

"Well," I said, giving in, "just don't make me sit next to Mr. Kinjo."

But as things turned out, that is exactly where I ended up on Thanksgiving Day.

IX

THE MINUTE WE GOT TO MRS. SUGINO'S ON THANKS-giving, Mama and I headed straight for the kitchen and left Papa and Joji to go talk to the others in the parlor. The house was already filled with the smell of sixteen wonderful pounds of roasting turkey, and I almost fainted from hunger then and there.

"Ooooh, Mrs. Sugino, it sure smells good," I said, the minute I saw her. "How much longer till it's done?"

Mrs. S. was washing some parsley, but she smiled and wiped her hands when we came in.

"Not too much longer, Rinko," she answered. "Mr. Kinjo helped me stuff the turkey last night and put it in the oven for me this morning."

"Why, how nice of him," Mama said, putting on her apron, "I can see he's going to be a fine helpful husband."

I was afraid Mama was going to start talking about his marriage to Teru, but thank goodness she didn't. I guess she was anxious to get on with fixing dinner. I could tell it made her nervous to see the big kitchen table littered with newspapers and not ready for our dinner.

"Why don't you set the table, Rinko?" she suggested. "But first find a place for this, will you?" And she handed me the pot of rice she'd cooked at home and brought all wrapped up in a blanket, like a baby, to keep warm.

I was looking around for a good place to put it when Mrs. S. told me to go put it under the quilt at the foot of her bed.

"That should keep it nice and warm till dinnertime," she said. "And while you're there, Rinko, will you get my good silverware?"

"From the bedroom?" I asked, puzzled.

"Yes, it's under the bed," she explained, as though that was where everybody kept their good silver. "There's a carton there marked 'Chinese noodles', but actually it's my good silver inside."

I thought maybe her good dishes might be under the bed too, in the carton marked "canned sardines," but it turned out they were in a cupboard in the laundry room. I had to get up on a stool and hand the dishes to Mrs. S. one by one. They looked slightly dusty to me, but Mrs. S. didn't bother to wash them like I knew Mama would, and I figured a little bit of dust wouldn't hurt us, especially if it was mixed up with turkey gravy.

Mama was busy putting the candied yams in the oven

and getting the peas and carrots ready to cook on top of the stove.

"There now," she said, beginning to relax. "I'll make the gravy when the turkey is done, and we'll be all ready."

Mama let me whip the cream for the pumpkin pie, and I began licking off the egg beater when I was done. I hadn't nearly finished curling my tongue around all the loops and curves of the beater when Mama stopped me.

"Mah, Rinko, such manners!" she scolded, and she shooed me out of the kitchen before I could object.

I know it wasn't only my manners she was worried about. I knew she wanted to have a private talk with Mrs. S. So I wandered into the parlor where I found a big surprise. All the cartons and books and magazines had been moved to one end of the room, and there was a nice big space in the middle for all us people.

"Hey, the parlor sure looks different!" I said. But nobody listened to me. Everybody was busy with conversations of their own, and Joji and Boku were playing checkers behind the sofa.

I'd promised Joji a licorice stick if he'd keep Boku out of my hair for the day. "Look on him as a challenge," I'd said. And good old Joji obliged, because he will do almost anything for a piece of licorice.

Whenever we go to the corner store to buy penny candy, he always chooses a licorice stick first, and then if he has another penny, he will get a butterscotch ball.

Personally, I can't stand licorice. I think it tastes like medicine, and I don't like having a black tongue. What I like best are red and green jujubes. Of course, they stick all over your teeth, and you finally have to stick a finger in your mouth to scrape them off. But I think they're worth it.

Now I heard Joji say to Boku, "Hey, you can't move the red king. He's mine."

And Boku answered, "Then I wanna switch colors. I like red."

"Well, ya can't switch once you've begun the game."

"Then I wanna start over!"

They almost sounded like Cal and me when he's trying to teach me how to play chess. I keep getting mixed up about the way the knight can jump, because it can do weird things like move up a square and over two or up two and over one.

Cal usually can't stand more than ten minutes of playing with me, and then he'll say, "You're impossible, Rink. I give up."

And then I'll say, "If you were a better teacher, maybe I could learn how to play!"

Mr. Sad Higa hadn't come downstairs yet, but Mr. Kinjo and Johnny were huddled over a game of *Shogi*, which is sort of like Japanese chess. But they didn't seem too interested in the game, because they were having a discussion about something.

I was glad the pile of magazines had been moved from the seat of the big armchair, because I discovered that if I sat in it and leaned way back, nobody noticed me, and I could hear everything the two men were saying.

"I really don't see much of a future for myself in America," Johnny said, sounding rather glum.

But Mr. Kinjo didn't agree with him. "It may not be the promised land we dreamed about," he said, "but this is where I want to make my home."

Johnny frowned. "You'll always be an outsider here, Kinjo. You know that, don't you? You'll always be a foreigner since the law won't allow Asians to become citizens."

Mr. Kinjo sighed. "Well, maybe not now," he said. "But I have hope things will change someday. I'm staking my future on this country."

He sounded like Papa, and I wished Johnny felt the same way. In fact I wished Papa was right there talking to Johnny, but Papa was on the other side of the room, trapped by Mr. Sugino, who was waving a big cigar in his face.

I'd only seen Mr. Sugino for a minute when we arrived, but now I had a chance to look him over without his knowing it. I leaned back and took a good look.

He was a tall, big-boned man, with a part right down the middle of his head, like a highway between two mounds of hair. He was wearing a black suit, with a gold watch chain hanging across his vest. But the suit looked as though it hadn't been pressed in quite a while.

His face was flushed, as if he'd already sampled some

plum wine, and the strange thing was I couldn't think of one animal that he reminded me of. I guess because there was something about him I didn't like, and I like most animals, except maybe snakes.

Mr. Sugino was leaning toward Papa, pouring words over him in a loud voice, like maybe he was trying to sell Papa some life insurance. I could tell Papa wasn't enjoying the conversation one bit and was sure he'd become his honest self any minute and put an end to the conversation.

I was trying real hard to hear what Papa was saying when I heard a voice say, "What are you doing in the corner all by yourself, Rinko?"

I looked up and it was Mr. Kinjo, who'd finished his game of *Shogi* with Johnny. This was the first time I'd talked to him since that awful night when I'd insulted him. He hadn't been home for supper on Saturdays because he now had a second job. Mrs. S. said he was trying to earn some extra money working as a sorter and marker at Mr. Sad Higa's laundry. He pulled up a chair and sat down beside me, making me squirm and pick at the fuzz balls on my sweater.

I noticed Mr. Kinjo had on his Sunday clothes. His suit was black, too, only *it* looked clean and pressed. His thick hair was slicked down with hair oil, and even his shoes were shined. In fact, he looked as though he was practicing for his wedding day.

I told him I was just waiting for dinner but couldn't think of anything else to say, so I told him about the stray dog that Auntie Hata recently adopted. She was keeping it, she said, because it understood when she talked to it in Japanese.

"He just walked into their house one day," I explained. "And Auntie Hata named him Mr. Gus Bailey after the mailman. She calls him Mr. Bailey. Isn't that a funny name for a dog?"

Mr. Kinjo smiled and nodded.

"She gave her compost pile a name, too," I added. "She calls it Freddie. So when she tells the kids to go feed Freddie with the garbage, people think she's talking about the dog."

I thought all this was fascinating, but I could see Mr. Kinjo didn't want to discuss Auntie Hata's dog or her compost pile. He probably knew all about them anyhow.

"I'm not always going to be a gardener, you know," he said, as though we were continuing a conversation we'd begun ten minutes before. "Someday I want to have a nursery of my own and specialize in growing carnations or maybe roses. I want to develop hybrids with colors no one has ever dreamed of before."

Then he told me how it really wasn't as impossible as it sounded, because there were other Japanese men who had become successful. Like the "Potato King," who grew potatoes in the Delta where nobody else could make anything grow. And like the man who discovered abalone in San Pedro and built up a big fishing industry down there.

"I want to leave my mark on this country, too," he said. "Maybe make it a better place because of something I've done. Do you understand?"

He looked eager and hopeful. And he sat up straight and tall in his chair.

Then suddenly he said, "I'm going to make Teru proud of me, Rinko. You just wait and see."

I realized then what Mr. Kinjo was doing. He was trying to make me understand that he would be a good husband to Teru. I wanted to say something nice to him this time, so I said, "That sounds swell, Mr. Kinjo. That sure is a wonderful dream."

But I couldn't say I thought he'd make Teru happy. And, thank goodness, just then Johnny Ochi came to rescue me.

"Ladies and gentlemen," he said, bowing with a flourish, "I've been asked to announce that dinner is served."

Then he crooked his elbow and gave me his arm, and we marched into the kitchen together. That was when a brilliant idea popped into my head.

By the time we'd finished dinner, I was sure my idea was perfect. Mr. Sad Higa and Mr. Kinjo were giving us a joint performance of *Shigin*, (a sort of Japanese chant), which Papa says is a highly refined art form. But it sounds to me like a dog howling in misery, and I absolutely cannot stand to listen to it.

Any time Papa tries to give us a performance of it at home, I stick my fingers in my ears and sing "Dixie" real loud so I can't hear him.

Of course, I couldn't do that at Mrs. Sugino's, so I

was suffering in silence. All my muscles were tensed up, and I was feeling like an ironing board when I happened to look at Johnny. He gave me a quick wink and rolled his eyeballs up to the ceiling to let me know he was suffering as much as I was.

That's when I knew he was a kindred soul, and I knew for double sure that *he* was the one who could save Teru. It was John Ochi, the Prince, who should ask Teru to marry him. I knew *he* was the one who could really make her happy, and I wondered why it had taken me so long to figure that out.

X

AS SOON AS I TOLD TK ABOUT MY BRILLIANT NEW idea, she began calling me every single day.

"Have you talked to Johnny yet?" she'd ask.

"Not yet."

"Well, why ever not?"

"Because he's got a part-time job at the Far East Cafe now, and he's never home."

"Well, you'd just better hurry up," TK would say. "Teru's going to be here real soon!"

"I know it!"

She certainly didn't have to remind me. I thought about it every single day. Then before I knew it, Teru was arriving, and Mama said her ship would dock in San Francisco on Friday. If I could just get Cal to drive me over to meet her ship, I thought, I could have a sort of sister-to-sister talk and tell her directly about John Ochi.

I pictured her giving me a big hug and saying, "Oh, thank you, Rinko. What a relief I won't have to marry Mr. Kinjo!"

I hurried outside to talk to Cal. He was helping Papa repair somebody's truck while Papa went to get some spare parts, and I could see Cal's scuffed shoes sticking out from underneath the truck.

I stood by his feet and yelled, "Hey, Cal. Come out a minute."

"Can't, Rink. I'm busy."

"How about in ten minutes then?"

"I'm busy all afternoon."

"Doing what?"

I could tell he was trying to think up a good excuse.

"I'm meeting Susie."

"Again? What for?"

Cal was hammering something and his feet jiggled every time he hit it.

"To do what?" I asked again, although I was pretty sure Cal would just tell me it was none of my business.

Instead, he yelled back, "We're eloping."

"What?"

I rushed to the other side of the truck so I could talk to his head instead of his feet. I got down on my hands and knees and bent my head sideways so I could see his face.

"Honest?" I screamed. "You and Susie are really going to elope?"

That certainly got Cal out from under the truck in a hurry.

"For pete's sake, Rink. Why don't you just get a loudspeaker and announce it to the whole neighborhood?" he asked.

But I kept right on yelling. "Why do you have to go off and elope? I wanted you to have a big church wedding! I wanted to see Susie all dressed up in a white satin wedding gown. Maybe she would've even let me be a bridesmaid. I wanted . . ."

That was when Cal clapped a greasy hand over my mouth.

"Good night, Rink, I was only kidding," he said. "You've been so darn wedding crazy these days, I thought I'd give you a little charge, that's all. Calm down. I was only joking."

Cal was right. I *had* been spouting off a lot about weddings lately. And I *had* been badgering Cal about whether he loved Susie enough to marry her.

"Sure I do," he'd said. "But we've both got to graduate from college first, and I've got to get a job, if somebody will hire me."

"What if you didn't have Susie?" I asked. "What if Mama and Papa arranged a marriage for you. Would you marry somebody you didn't love?"

Cal ignored me.

"Well, would you?"

"What a stupid question, Rink. Of course I wouldn't."

"Neither would I. I don't think anybody should have to marry somebody they don't love, do you, Cal? Do you?"

"Of course, it's better if you love each other," he agreed. "But sometimes it works out even if you don't." He sounded like Auntie Hata.

When I'd simmered down and had Cal's full and

undivided attention, I told him I thought it would be great if we went to meet Teru's ship.

"Let's go, huh, Cal?" I asked.

He gave me one of his don't-you-have-any-brains-at-all looks and said, "It's not your place to be there, Rink."

"Why not?" I wanted to know. "I'm Auntie Hata's summer daughter. It's like my sister is arriving from Japan, and I should be there to meet her. Besides," I added, "I have something important to tell her. We could pick up Auntie Hata and take her too."

But Cal told me that if anybody should go meet Teru, it was Mr. Kinjo, and he was the one who should take Auntie Hata, not Cal and me.

"They'll manage without you, Rink," he said. And he slid back under the truck and began hammering again.

So I asked Mama if Papa couldn't take all of us, but she said the same thing as Cal.

"We'll meet Teru on Sunday," Mama promised. "I'll pack a nice lunch for all of us, and we'll go to Mrs. Hata's right after church."

"Swell, Mama," I said. But I certainly couldn't wait until Sunday for news of Teru.

The minute I got to Mrs. S.'s for my Japanese lesson on Saturday, I asked. "Is Teru here? Did she get here all right? Is she nice?"

"Yes, yes, and yes," Mrs. S. said, but she didn't look a bit happy, so I asked if her wrist still hurt. It was finally out of a cast now, but Mrs. S. kept her arm bent as though it had gotten used to being that way.

"My wrist is all right, Rinko," she said, "and Teru is here safe and sound. I have never seen Mr. Kinjo look so happy."

But Mrs. S. looked as though she had a bad toothache.

"Then how come you look so sad?" I asked. "Did Boku do something awful? Did you send him to his room?" I asked looking around for a sign of him.

"No, he's gone off with Mr. Higa to feed the ducks at Lake Merritt," she explained. And then she burst into tears.

That certainly wasn't anything to cry about. I would have thought she'd be glad to get Boku out of the house.

"What's wrong, Mrs. Sugino?" I asked. "Why are you crying?"

She dabbed at her eyes and said, "Ah, Rinko, if only I could tell you."

I wished she would. But she just said, "I certainly hope you never have the problems I've had. I hope you marry a man who is reliable and trustworthy."

I was surprised to hear her talk like that. "Why? Isn't Mr. Sugino? Reliable and trustworthy, I mean?"

"If you only knew," she answered. "That man deceived me from the moment he first wrote to ask me to marry him," she said miserably. "He was dishonest enough to send me the photograph of a younger and more handsome man and pass it off as himself! He . . ."

She stopped suddenly, as though she realized she shouldn't be talking to me like that. She waved her hand in the air as if she was erasing her words and said, "Never mind, Rinko. Just forget what I told you."

"Don't worry, I won't tell anybody," I promised. "I've never told anybody about your other secret."

The other secret I knew was that Mrs. S. kept a wad of money rolled up in her bosom, under her corset. I'd helped her get some of it out in a hurry one day when her arm was still in a cast.

"Come help me unbutton my blouse," she'd said, and we went to her bedroom and sat on the edge of the creaky sagging brass bed.

"Rinko, you are the only person in this world who knows about my little secret bank account," she'd said, with a little giggle. "Not even my husband knows about it."

I wondered why she'd want to hide money from her husband. I knew Mama would never do a thing like that to Papa.

But I promised, "I'll never tell a soul. Cross my heart and hope to die." And I hadn't. That was the kind of promise you had to keep.

"I won't even tell Mama or Papa what you just said," I promised once more to make her feel better.

Mrs. S. dried her eyes and patted me on the shoulder. "I know I can trust you, Rinko," she said.

But she still didn't tell me why she was so upset. She just took me into the kitchen, opened my Japanese book to Lesson Seven and said, "Now, please read, Rinko." It was as though she'd suddenly turned into a teacher and stopped being my friend.

I could hardly concentrate on my lesson, even when she told me the interesting fact that the character for "woman" 女 written three times 姦 was the word for "noisy."

"That's not fair," I said, thinking how noisy Papa and Cal could be when they started arguing. "It ought to be three men."

But Mrs. S. didn't seem particularly interested in my opinion. As soon as my hour was up, she said she had to go out on an important errand.

"Shall I stay and help you get supper?" I asked.

Mrs. S. shook her head. "No, thank you, Rinko. I can manage pretty well now. You run along home."

I was dying to stay and find out what was troubling her, but what can you do when you're not wanted. I said good-bye and left.

Pretty soon I forgot about Mrs. S. and thought again about Teru. In just twenty-four hours I'd be meeting her, and then I could finally tell her about the handsome young husband I'd picked out for her.

XI

"CAN'T YOU GO ANY FASTER, PAPA? I ASKED.

We were almost at Auntie Hata's in East Oakland, but the closer we got, the worse the road became. So Papa had to slow down, which pleased Mama. She is so nervous about riding with Papa, she refuses to sit up in front with him and always sits in back with me.

I guess it's because of the accident we had once when Papa didn't look where he was going and smacked right into a telephone pole. It was pretty scary, all right. Mama got a huge bump on her head and I banged my forehead on the back of the front seat.

Now every time we get near another car or Papa starts going too fast, Mama yells, "Look out, Papa!" and she grabs my arm.

"Ow, Mama," I say, pulling my arm away. But five minutes later, she will do it again. It's a wonder my arm isn't black and blue from all the times it's been grabbed by Mama in the back seat of our car.

Joji always sits up in front with Papa, watching like

a hawk, so he'll know what to do when he can drive. He thinks it's going to be any day now. When I remind him that he's still only a child, he says, "Well, Cal learned how to drive when he was twelve, didn't he?" And it's true, he did.

Joji's favorite place to sit and study is in our Model T. Or sometimes I see him pretending to drive, stepping on the clutch or the brake or handling the steering wheel, and humming under his breath like Papa does, as though that was part of knowing how to drive.

I know what I am going to do on the day that Joji actually does drive. I am going to stay out of our car. Period.

"There's Auntie Hata's!" I hollered the minute we bumped over the railroad tracks and I could see the shabby old house with the fields in back. There wasn't a sign of the cucumbers that had grown there in the summer, and the weeds had taken over, growing tall and green from the first rains of winter.

I could see two kites soaring up in the sky and knew Auntie Hata's two boys had already gotten their kites up with a good wind from the bay.

The minute we rattled into the front yard, Joji jumped out of the car. "Hey, Zenny! Abu!" he yelled, and ran toward the fields behind the house.

"Don't you want to meet Teru?" I shouted at him, but he didn't even bother to answer.

Auntie Hata and Teru came out to meet us as soon as they heard our car drive up. They were smiling and waving as they hurried down the front steps.

Teru was wearing a beautiful green silk kimono decorated with white peonies and butterflies, and her wide brocade sash was flecked with gold. I was sure it must be her very best kimono.

She was slim and not very tall, and her straight black hair was parted in the middle and gathered in back. Her pale clear skin was as smooth as a porcelain teacup, and her dark eyes looked very wise.

In fact, she was so pretty, she reminded me of a Japanese doll. Not the kind Mama used to make for me out of cornhusks, dressed in paper kimonos, but like the doll in the glass case on Mrs. Sugino's mantel. The one with real hair, dressed in a kimono of silk crepe.

The minute I saw Teru, I knew she and Johnny Ochi would be perfect together. The movie-actor prince and the Japanese doll! TK's mother would certainly be proud of me for arranging such an ideal match, and I could already picture Teru in a beautiful wedding gown with a huge long train.

I wanted to rush right up and tell her I was going to save her, but I suddenly got tongue-tied. I just stood there like a ninny and stared at her.

"Well, Rinko, say hello to my daughter Teru," Auntie Hata said with a big smile.

Auntie Hata was all dressed up too, in a black wool skirt and a neatly ironed white blouse instead of one of the faded, wrinkled cotton dresses she usually wore. She also had two tortoise shell combs stuck in her hair. I'd never seen her wear anything in her hair before, and the combs were pushed in sort of crooked, not looking quite right. I guessed they were probably a present Teru had brought her from Japan.

Teru bowed to Mama and Papa and said all the nice polite things you're supposed to say when you meet people. And of course Mama and Papa did exactly the same.

"Well, where is Mr. Kinjo?" Papa asked eagerly. "Where is the happy bridegroom?"

Auntie Hata's face grew solemn then, and she said, "I'm afraid he can't come today. There's been an emergency at Mrs. Sugino's."

I wondered if it had anything to do with why Mrs. S. seemed so upset and worried when I saw her on Saturday.

"She hasn't had another accident, has she?" Mama asked.

Auntie Hata drew her aside and whispered something in her ear, and now Mama looked solemn and worried too.

"Hey, Rinko, wanna fly kites?" Zenny called to me from out back.

But nothing in the world could have pried me away from what was going on or from being with Teru.

"Not now," I yelled back.

I tried hard to hear what Auntie Hata was saying, but she took Mama's arm and they moved away with Papa. All of them looked serious and were talking in whispers.

Teru smiled and held out her hand toward me. "Let's go inside," she said, speaking in simple Japanese so I could understand. "We don't care what the others are talking about, do we?"

I really did, but I shook my head and caught her hand. And suddenly I had this warm, good feeling, as though I was linked up with a real honest-to-goodness sister. I've wanted a sister so badly, sometimes I tell Mama she should have kept right on having more babies until she'd had another girl to keep me company.

Then Mama will say, "But maybe you would have had three or four younger brothers then instead of just one."

And I have to say, "Well, in that case, thank goodness you stopped with Joji."

I really don't remember much about lunch. I know everybody was talking about how wonderful it was that Teru was finally home and would soon be marrying Mr. Kinjo. And nobody mentioned the emergency at Mrs. Sugino's again. I would have asked about it, except I was so busy wondering how I was going to tell Teru about John Ochi that I couldn't think about anything else.

As soon as lunch was over, Abu poked me in the arm.

"Now do ya?" he asked.

"Do I what?"

"Wanna fly kites?" he asked impatiently.

Any other day, I would have been out of the house in a minute, racing out to the fields to get my kite soaring up in the sky before any of the boys did. But today, I wasn't the Rinko I'd been when I was staying at Auntie Hata's during the summer. Today I had more important things to do. Grown up things. And suddenly Abu just seemed like a little kid.

"You go on outside and play," I said to him.

I watched Abu rush out after Joji and Zenny, banging the screen door behind him, and for just a second I wanted to go along. But when I looked at Teru, I knew what I really wanted to do.

It was almost as though she'd read my mind, because she said, "Would you like to go upstairs to my room with me?"

Would I! I jumped up from the table, and fortunately Mama didn't tell me I should clear the table and help with the dishes. I guess she had other things on her mind too, because she and Auntie Hata had their heads together. They were probably either making plans for the wedding or talking about the mysterious emergency, I thought.

I followed Teru up the creaky old stairs, watching as she pattered softly in her pale gray sandals. She was so graceful, she almost seemed to be doing a Japanese dance as she moved. I guess Auntie Hata was really proud that Teru had turned out to be exactly the kind of fine Japanese lady she'd always wanted her to be.

When we got to her room, Teru pushed open the door and motioned for me to go in first.

"*Dozo*, please," she said with a slight bow.

I felt as though I'd just been invited into the parlor of a princess.

XII

AS SOON AS I WAS IN TERU'S ROOM, I SAW THE OLD familiar bureau with the chipped paint and the narrow cot where I'd slept when I was staying with Auntie Hata.

"This is the very room I slept in all during August," I said in my best Japanese.

"I know," Teru answered. "Mother told me how much you helped her. She said you were like a daughter to her."

"Uh-huh, her summer daughter. But now she's got you for a permanent daughter and that's even better."

Teru nodded. "I'm so grateful to Mr. Kinjo for making it possible," she said, and she motioned for me to sit beside her on the squeaky cot.

I was going crazy trying to think of the Japanese words to tell her what I wanted to say. I can understand Japanese pretty well, but it's still hard for me to speak it.

"Are you, uh . . . will you be, uh . . ."

I thought I'd asked her if she would be happy. But I guess I made a mistake, because suddenly Teru covered her mouth with her hand and began to giggle.

"You asked if I would be wrinkled (*shi-wa-kucha*), but I think you meant to ask if I would be happy (*shi-ya-wasé*)," she explained. And then she told me she had studied English all through high school.

"Shall we speak in English?" she asked.

"Oh, yes. Thank goodness!" I wished she'd told me earlier.

I had a million things I wanted to ask her. I was so curious about how she felt, being shipped off to live with her grandparents when she was only a baby.

"Weren't you mad at your mama for leaving you in Japan?" I asked. "Weren't you lonely? Didn't you miss your mama and papa and wonder what your brothers were like? Golly, if it were me," I rushed on, "I'd rather have stayed with my own family even if I had to live on a farm and pick strawberries in the sun and wear grubby clothes and dig weeds and even use an outhouse!"

I finally gave Teru a chance to answer, and she spoke slowly and carefully in English.

"When I was about your age, I *was* angry at my mama, even if I knew she only wanted the best for me," Teru said. "But remember, my grandparents were like parents to me. And one day my grandmother said, 'Teru, you can go on using your energy to be angry all your life and be a bitter, sour person. Or you can accept your life as it is and enjoy it.' Well, I thought about that for a long time," Teru went on, "and one day, I just stopped being angry and decided to accept who I was. Do you understand?"

"Sort of," I said, trying.

"For nineteen years I was a good Japanese. But now I'm back where I was born, and I intend to become a good American."

Teru stopped talking then and smiled at me. I thought what she'd just said sounded a little like Mr. Kinjo. And that reminded me of the important thing I had to say to her.

"Listen, Teru," I began. I scratched my nose and wiggled my ears like I do when I'm really nervous about something.

"I have somebody much better for you than Mr. Kinjo. He's young and handsome and his name is John Junichi Ochi. He lives at Mrs. Sugino's, too, and he wants to be an engineer someday, like my brother Cal. But he might become an actor! Wouldn't that be exciting? Being married to an actor, I mean.

"Anyway, I'm going to tell him he should propose to you so you won't have to marry Mr. Kinjo. Then you and Johnny can live happily ever after—like in a fairy tale. Won't that be wonderful? You'll be perfect together!"

I finally stopped jabbering and took a deep breath. My heart was bouncing inside my chest like a rubber ball, and I could hardly wait for Teru to tell me how happy I'd made her.

But instead of looking pleased, she looked as though I'd thrown a glass of cold water in her face.

"Oh, Rinko," she said. "You mustn't talk like that. Mr. Kinjo is a good man and I'm already promised to him."

"But you don't even know him," I interrupted. "And I really think it's OK to change your mind about something *this* important, even if you did promise."

I was surprised when Teru told me he wasn't exactly a stranger since they'd been writing to each other for several months. But I was even more surprised when Teru just stopped listening to me.

She got up and pulled out an old leather suitcase from under her cot. When she opened it, I could see it was filled with a lot of kimonos all folded neatly and wrapped in soft rice paper.

She felt carefully in each corner of the suitcase and finally pulled out a small box. She held it out to me saying, "I brought this especially for you, Rinko."

In Japan it's not polite to open a gift the minute you get it, but I couldn't wait. I tore off the wrapping and when I opened the box, I found a small Japanese doll. It had real hair and was dressed in a flowered silk kimono with a brocade sash.

"Oh, Teru," I said, "she looks just like you. She's beautiful! And you're too beautiful for Mr. Kinjo," I blurted out, becoming my honest self again. "You've got to meet Johnny, and I know you'll change your mind."

Teru just reached over and patted my hand. "I thought you might enjoy the doll, Rinko," she said.

Then she pushed her suitcase back under the cot, smoothed the wrinkles from her kimono and said, "Now

I must go downstairs and make fresh tea for everyone. Why don't you go outside and play with the boys?"

I was flabbergasted and utterly speechless. Teru had talked to me exactly the way I'd talked to Abu earlier, and I realized then that she thought of me the way I thought of Abu or even Boku. Like a little kid.

I felt as though a sand castle I'd worked so hard to build had just been washed out by the tide, and I could almost hear Cal saying, "Didn't I tell you to mind your own business, Rink?"

Gosh darn it, Teru, I thought miserably, you just ruined the wonderful happy ending I had all planned for you and Johnny.

XIII

IT WAS A GOOD THING CHRISTMAS VACATION BEGAN the next day, because I was in a lousy mood after my big flop with Teru, and I certainly didn't feel like going to school.

"Let's go Christmas shopping," I suggested to TK.

I was all ready to give up on Teru, but TK wouldn't let me.

We were at the handkerchief counter at Hink's Department Store, and I was trying to decide between a lavender and a rose scented sachet for Mama, when TK brought up the subject again.

"If Teru ends up being miserable the rest of her life like Mrs. Sugino, it'll be all your fault, you know," she said out of the clear blue.

I immediately stopped sniffing sachets and said, "Hey, wait a minute. How do you know Mrs. S. is miserable?"

I'd known something was wrong, of course, but nobody had told me anything. TK's mother, however, is willing to share her secrets, and TK almost always passes them on to me.

"Mama said there's big trouble at her house," TK said, her eyes widening.

"Like what?" I asked. "Tell me!"

"Like Mr. Sugino's terrible affliction and what he just did."

I remembered Mrs. S. had told me he wasn't reliable or trustworthy, but I also remembered I'd promised not to tell. So I kept quiet and hoped TK would just keep on talking. And sure enough, she did.

She leaned close and whispered in my ear. "He drinks too much, and he loves to gamble. Mama said he gambles at card games and at the race track and just gambles away all their money, so poor Mrs. Sugino hardly has enough to run their house."

That explained a lot about Mrs. S. I thought about the worried look on her face the last time I saw her and about the secret bank account she kept in her bosom. It also explained the little things she did to save money, like cooking her rice with less water so people wouldn't eat as much.

"If the rice is too soft," she'd explained, "everyone will take bigger mouthfuls and eat more of it."

Maybe, I thought, that was why she saved so many things. Because she didn't know when she'd run out of money and not be able to buy anything. She'd told me once that she charged seven dollars a month for room and twenty dollars for board and that barely covered her expenses.

"I knew there was something about Mr. Sugino I didn't like," I said. "But what's the big trouble right now?"

"It's really awful," TK said, pulling me away from the counter so the saleslady wouldn't hear. "Promise you won't tell?"

"OK," I said, but I had my feet crossed, because I knew if it was something *really* terrible, I'd have to tell Mama and Papa, although they probably knew already. That was probably the emergency they'd been whispering about at Auntie Hata's.

"Well, this time Mr. Sugino didn't just gamble his own money," TK went on. "He took all the money one of their boarders had saved up to take back to Japan and said he'd double it for him."

"That must be Mr. Sad Higa," I said. "But if he doubled his money that was good, wasn't it?"

"But he didn't!" TK was having a hard time keeping her voice down now. "He lost every penny of it. All fifteen hundred dollars!"

"You mean Mr. Sad Higa has no money left now to take home to Japan?"

TK nodded solemnly. "Not one cent! All he has left is his steamship ticket home."

I thought how poor Mr. Sad Higa had ironed his life away in that damp dark laundry, trying to save up money for his family in Japan. And I remembered how happy he'd looked the night he'd talked about going home at last. How could Mr. Sugino do such an awful thing to Mr. Sad Higa? I was furious with him.

"What a . . . a . . . a skunk!" I said. I'd finally found the right animal for Mr. Sugino.

If I could've remembered some good swear words I would have used those too, but just when I needed some, I couldn't think of a good one. Besides, the saleslady was getting impatient. She was glaring at me and tapping her fingers on top of the counter.

"Well, young lady," she said. "Do you want the sachet or not?"

"I'll take the lavender one," I said, just because that was the one I had in my hand.

I was so shocked by what I'd just heard, I couldn't think of anything else. And I'd certainly forgotten all about Teru. But not TK.

"So you see," she went on, picking up where she'd left off, "you'd better do something about Teru, or she'll end up married to the wrong man and be miserable the rest of her life. Just like Mrs. Sugino!"

Well, I certainly didn't want that to happen. I felt my heart melting again for beautiful Teru. But I just didn't know what to do next.

When I got home, Mama gave me the answer. "Will you take some of our eggs to Mrs. Sugino today?" she asked. "I've baked some bread for her too."

I was ready to do anything for Mrs. S. then. It also occurred to me that I might run into Johnny and have one last go at trying to change Teru's mind. So I told Mama, sure I'd go. I guess she was surprised I didn't even give her an argument, especially since Papa was out collecting laundry and couldn't drive me over.

All the way to Oakland on the streetcar, I kept wondering what I should say when I saw Mrs. S. Should I pretend I didn't know anything about what her husband had done? Or should I say how awful I thought he was? Or what?

But when I got to her house, the first words that came out of my mouth were, "Oh, my gosh!"

What I saw was a pile of boxes, two old suitcases and some clothes, all stacked at the curb in front of the house. And there was Boku sitting at the top of the front steps sniffling and rubbing his eyes.

"Hey, Boku, what's going on?" I asked.

He didn't throw any sticky half-eaten pieces of bread at me, or stick out his tongue, or do any of the other nasty things he'd done to me before.

He just took one look at me and began to wail.

I sat down beside him and tried asking again. "What's wrong, Boku? Tell me."

But all he could say was, "Waaaaah!"

XIV

EVEN A BRAT NEEDS TO BE LOVED AND COMFORTED when he's feeling as bad as Boku was—especially when he has such a horrible papa. So I put my arm around him. Instead of fighting me off like I thought he would, he buried his head in my lap and kept on crying.

"Well, whatever it is," I said, "it can't be that bad." And I tried to think of something to cheer him up.

"Want to hear something funny, Boku?" I asked. "My brother Cal told me about this lake in Massachusetts with a really crazy name the Indians gave it. It's called, CHARGOGGAGOGG MANCHAUGAGOGG CHAUBUNAGUNGAMAUG. You want to know what it means?"

Boku didn't answer, but he stopped crying, so I told him.

"It means, 'You fish on your side, I fish on mine, nobody fish in the middle.' Cal swears that's an absolutely true fact and it kept the Indians from fighting. Isn't that funny?"

I guess that cheered him up all right, because Boku suddenly sat up, and he said, "Papa's gone!"

Just then Mrs. S. came out of the house and threw a batch of neckties down toward the pile of stuff at the curb. They came flying over my head and landed all over the sidewalk. I was surprised she wasn't saving them.

"There!" she said. "I'm free now of him and all his possessions! The Salvation Army is welcome to them."

Her face was red and her eyes were puffed up from crying, and her hair was sort of flying around her face.

"Mrs. Sugino, you look awful!" I said, acting like Papa and blurting out the honest truth. "What happened, anyway?"

Mrs. S. smiled when she noticed me, and her face lit up. "I've thrown him out of the house, that's what," she said. "I should have done it years ago."

"Who?" I asked, although I had a pretty good idea who she was talking about.

"That miserable, no good, stupid husband of mine!" she answered. "That scoundrel . . . that weasel . . . that . . . that . . ."

"Skunk?" I offered.

"Yes, that skunk!"

After all that, I certainly couldn't pretend I didn't know what had happened.

"I think it's awful, what he did to poor Mr. Higa," I said. "I'm glad you threw him out!"

I felt proud of Mrs. S. for being strong and brave and getting rid of her skunk-husband.

"I told him I never wanted to see him again—ever,"

she said fiercely. "He has brought shame on all of us. On me . . . on Boku . . . on the name of Sugino."

Whenever Mama and Papa have a fight, they usually try not to argue in front of us kids. So I was surprised when Mrs. S. let me see her anger without trying to hide it. But I was glad, because it made me feel like she'd accepted me as an equal—a real friend—and not just a child.

I waited to give her the eggs until she'd calmed down, because I was afraid she'd throw them one by one on top of Mr. Sugino's stuff. I guess that would have made her feel good, but I didn't think Mama would want her eggs wasted on Mr. S.

When Mrs. S. asked me to come inside, Boku wouldn't come with us.

"No," he said stubbornly. "I'm gonna wait here for my papa."

I looked at Mrs. S. to see what she would do. But she just shrugged and said, "Let him be. I'll have a talk with him later on."

So I followed Mrs. S. into the kitchen where she was cooking a pot of red *azuki* beans. She gave them a good stir with a wooden spoon and then came to sit with me at the kitchen table.

"What in the world am I going to do about poor Mr. Higa?" she asked.

I hadn't the faintest notion. But Mrs. S. wasn't really asking me, she was just talking out loud to herself.

"I'm going to return his money to him if it's the last thing I do," she said. "I am certainly not going to let that poor man board his ship next month without a penny in his pocket."

"Do you have enough in your, you know . . . ?" I asked, patting my chest.

"Oh, no, that's all gone," she said with a long sigh.

"Then how about borrowing from the Japanese Association? Don't they always help?"

But Mrs. S. shook her head. "I'm too ashamed to go to them," she said.

"Then how?" I asked.

"That's just it, Rinko," Mrs. S. answered. "How?"

The two of us sat there at the kitchen table, as though we were waiting for a fairy godmother to appear with a pot of gold. But when the back door opened, it was only Mr. Kinjo.

"Not much gardening to do this time of year," he said, taking off his jacket, "so I decided to take the rest of the day off."

He put a big bag of buttered popcorn on the table saying, "Here's a treat for Boku."

It smelled so good, I was wishing he'd offer me some. But all he did was ask if I'd come for another Japanese lesson.

"No, only to bring some fresh eggs from Mama," I explained, and then I asked him if Johnny would be home soon.

"Oh, didn't you know?" he asked. "Johnny left last night for a trip to Los Angeles."

"He did? What for?"

"Well, it's Christmas vacation, you know, and he's

been saving up to go to Hollywood to meet the famous Japanese actor, Sessue Hayakawa."

I was flabbergasted. How could Johnny just go off like that when Mrs. S. was so upset and poor Mr. Sad Higa was left penniless? Didn't he want to stay and at least try to cheer them up a little?

"Well, I guess I can't talk to him then," I said lamely.

It was a good thing nobody asked why I wanted to see Johnny in the first place, because now, suddenly, I wasn't so sure I had anything to say to him. I felt this terrible disappointment coming over me, as though somebody had just wrapped me up in a big, wet, cold blanket. I couldn't believe Johnny had just walked out on his friends when they needed him most.

It was almost as though Mr. Kinjo could read my mind, the way Mama does.

"Johnny is still young, Rinko," he said, trying to explain things to me. "He has a lot of big dreams inside his head, and he *did* have this trip planned for a long time, you know."

But didn't Johnny care at all about anybody here, I wondered? What happened to my handsome prince? I always thought a prince came galloping to the rescue when there was big trouble. A prince didn't just leave his friends when they needed him and go off to Los Angeles, for heaven's sake.

I felt all mixed up inside—like I'd dumped everything from my bureau drawer out on my bed and needed to sort things out. I knew I had a lot of thinking to do. But I heard Mrs. S. asking me to go get Boku.

"Tell him Mr. Kinjo's brought him some popcorn," she said. "That should bring him inside."

"OK," I said. And even before I got to the front door, I yelled, "Hey, Boku, there's hot buttered popcorn!"

But when I opened the door, Boku was gone. I ran down the steps and looked up and down the street. There wasn't a sign of him. I rushed back inside and looked in the parlor and called to him upstairs.

"Hey, Boku!" I hollered.

But all I heard was water dripping in the basin in the upstairs hall.

"Mrs. Sugino, he's gone!" I yelled, rushing back into the kitchen. "Boku's disappeared!"

XV

I NEVER SAW ANYBODY MOVE SO FAST. MR. KINJO jumped up from the table, grabbed his jacket, and said, "I'll find him, Mrs. Sugino. Don't you worry. He can't have gone far." And he dashed off.

Mrs. S. wanted to make sure Boku wasn't hiding somewhere in the house, so I helped her look everywhere. I looked in the closets, yelling, "Boku!" at all the clothes and junk inside. I also looked under the beds, but all I saw were puffy dustballs. I even went out to the backyard and looked inside the woodshed.

"Come out this instant!" I shouted.

But Boku wasn't anywhere.

Mrs. S. was sitting at the kitchen table, with her head in her hands, as though she was trying to hold in all the terrible thoughts that were gathering inside.

"Oh, Rinko," she said. "I should have talked to him right away. I should have explained everything, so he would understand. Suppose something terrible happens to him?"

"It won't," I said.

But actually I was thinking this was the second bad thing to happen to her after what her husband did, and now there might be one more.

"I'll call Papa," I said.

But Mrs. S. wouldn't let me. "Not just yet," she said. "First I want to check our street carefully before I bother your papa and mama. I've caused them enough worry already."

So we both put on our coats and went out in front. Mrs. S. headed in one direction and I went in the other.

"Be sure you ask about Boku at each shop," she told me.

I started by going into the little Chinese grocery store and found an old man with a long gray beard sitting beside a crate of shiny eggplants. I asked him if he'd seen Boku.

"You mean little Japanese boy?" he asked.

I nodded.

"Him look like little *sumo* wrestler?"

"That's the one."

The old man shook his head. "No see today," he said. "No see."

I got the same answer in the shop with all the skinned rabbits hanging in the window. When I got to the corner, I really didn't want to go into the pawn shop, but I remembered what Mrs. S. said, so I went in.

A little bell rang when I opened the door, and I saw a lady with a lot of frizzy red hair sitting behind the counter. She had huge gold earrings dangling from her ears, and rings on just about every finger except her thumbs.

"Well, well," she said, looking me over carefully, "brought me something nice, have you?"

I shook my head. "I'm looking for a little boy," I explained.

"I've got a lot of things in here," she said, glancing around, "but no little kids. Nope, nobody's brought me one of those. At least, not yet."

She seemed to think that was pretty funny and was still laughing when I went out the door.

I crossed the street then and asked at the tailor's and the tiny dusty herb shop. But nobody had seen Boku.

When I got back to the house, Mrs. Sugino said the same thing. "He's just vanished," she said, and she sank down wearily on the top step. I sat beside her, and we both stared at Mr. Sugino's stuff still piled up on the curb.

Mrs. S. shivered and pulled her coat collar up around her throat.

"If only it were springtime," she said sadly. "If only I could feel the sun on my back and smell the sweetness of jasmine in the air."

It was like she was longing for something nice from the past to hold on to, now that her life had turned so bleak.

I wanted so much to make her feel better that I said, "Maybe if you closed your eyes and thought real hard about jasmine, you could smell it."

Mrs. S. didn't make fun of me. "Do you think so?" she asked.

She closed her eyes real tight and took a deep long breath.

"Is it working?"

"Not yet."

"Maybe it'll work better if we both do it."

I closed my eyes tight too and thought of the sweet smell of jasmine filling the summer air at dusk. I took a huge deep breath and smelled . . . hot dogs!

"You can stop praying now," Mr. Kinjo said, thinking that's what we were doing. "I've brought him back. He'd gone all the way to 14th Street."

We both opened our eyes, and there they were, Boku and Mr. Kinjo. Boku was stuffing a hot dog in his mouth and acting as though nothing unusual had happened at all.

"Boku!" Mrs. S. shouted, reaching out to him. But Boku pulled away from her.

"Ah, you're angry with me, aren't you?" she said with a sigh. "Well, that's all right, Boku. You need to have somebody to be mad at, too, and it might as well be me. We'll have a talk later on."

"Thank goodness you weren't the second bad thing," I said to Boku.

"Whachew mean?" he asked.

"Never mind," I answered. I wasn't about to explain to him my theory about bad things coming in threes. Besides, I thought, maybe I was wrong about that anyway.

I noticed Mr. Kinjo was holding a brown sack, and he held it out to Mrs. S. saying he'd brought back hot dogs for all of us to have for supper.

"Supper!" I shouted. "I've got to get home or Mama will think something awful's happened to me."

Mr. Kinjo said in that case, he'd drive me home in his truck and he gave me one of the hot dogs to take home with me.

It was absolutely impossible for me to sit in Mr. Kinjo's truck holding a perfectly good hot dog oozing with ketchup and mustard and all kinds of good smells and not eat it. So I munched on it all the way home, which worked out fine, because I couldn't talk with my mouth full, and Mr. Kinjo did all the talking.

He didn't say anything about himself or Teru until he dropped me off in front of our house. Then he said, "See you at the party next Sunday."

"What party?" I asked.

"Oh, didn't your mama tell you? Mrs. Hata is having a party next Sunday. It was supposed to be a celebration for Teru and me, but now it isn't such a happy time for anyone, is it?"

Mr. Kinjo stopped talking for a minute. Then he said almost to himself, "Well, maybe everything will work out after all."

I didn't know what he was talking about, but I didn't want to ask. Besides, I knew I'd find out on Sunday.

XVI

ANY OTHER TIME, IF CHRISTMAS EVE AND SUNDAY and a party had all come together on the same day, I would have been beside myself with joy and excitement. But this year, Christmas got sort of pushed aside because of the Big Trouble at Mrs. Sugino's, and nobody felt much like celebrating.

Still, Auntie Hata wanted to have her party for Teru and Mr. Kinjo right after church, just like she'd been planning for weeks.

"After all," she said, "we do have much to celebrate in spite of everything."

And Mama said she was absolutely right. We were all invited, of course, and even Cal said he'd go. I think he was curious to meet Teru after all the talking I'd done about her.

Personally, I was feeling kind of glum about everything. I was mad at Mrs. Sugino's skunk-husband for causing all the trouble in the first place. But I was almost as mad at Johnny Ochi for being such a big disappointment to me.

"He's absolutely ruined everything," I told TK. "How can I arrange a match for somebody who isn't even here—especially when that somebody has just walked out on all his friends!"

"You mean Teru's stuck with Mr. Kinjo then?" she asked.

"I guess so," I said. Then I added, "At least he's here and he's working real hard to help Mrs. S. find enough money to pay back Mr. Sad Higa."

I was a little surprised to find myself saying nice things about Mr. Kinjo, and I guess TK was too. She couldn't seem to think of anything more to say then. Or maybe she was getting just plain bored with trying to save Teru, because suddenly she dropped the subject entirely.

"You know what I really want for Christmas?" she asked. "A gold chain with a tiny heart-shaped locket on it. What do you want?"

But Christmas was very different at our house this year. Cal, Joji, and I decided to skip giving presents to each other, and we even skipped having a Christmas tree so we could put the money instead into the fund Papa was collecting for Mr. Higa. In fact, I even offered to let Papa have some money from my going-to-college jar.

"I have almost thirteen dollars in it now," I told him. "I could give him some of that."

But Papa said he didn't think Mr. Higa would want me to do that.

"Don't worry, Rinko," he told me. "We'll work something out. We're asking everybody at church to help too, if they can."

But Sunday morning I heard Mama and Papa talking together in the kitchen, and I knew they hadn't been able to raise much money.

"Times are hard," Papa was saying. "Most people barely have enough to pay the rent and feed their families."

"I know," Mama agreed. "I'm afraid nobody has much money to spare these days."

I guessed we were pretty much in the same boat ourselves. Mama and Papa don't say much about our money problems, but I know for a fact that Papa is just managing to pay the bills. And Mama doesn't put as much meat into the stew as she used to.

I was afraid the party at Auntie Hata's was going to be as dismal as a cold foggy day, especially since Mrs. S. and Mr. Sad Higa were going to be there too. They certainly didn't have anything to be happy about.

Still, when we got to Auntie Hata's, she seemed to have enough happiness to go around for everybody.

"Welcome, welcome," she beamed at us. "Rinko, how nice to have your whole family here today. I do think this is the happiest Christmas of my entire life."

Both she and Teru were wearing their best clothes again. This time Teru had on a bright blue kimono with white cranes flying over it, and I thought she'd probably chosen it because cranes symbolize good fortune. She seemed to fit right into the Hata family, and already she was acting like a big sister, telling Zenny and Abu to go wash their hands before lunch. I hardly recognized them with their hair combed down and both of them in their good knickers and clean white shirts.

As soon as Joji and I arrived, Zenny and Abu steered us toward the kitchen table that Auntie Hata had moved into the parlor. It was covered with the same pink crepe paper she'd used for the celebration at the dormitory, but this time she'd folded red and green paper cranes for the decorations. Abu, however, wasn't interested in the decorations.

"Lookit the big fish," he said, pointing at the platter in the center of the table.

It certainly was big all right, with its tail and fins spread out fanlike. Another symbol of good luck. The fish seemed to be staring at me with white pearly eyes, and for a minute I felt sorry for it sitting there, all broiled and crisp, instead of swimming free and alive in the bay.

"It weighs over fifteen pounds," Zenny said proudly, and he told us how one of the men at Auntie Hata's dormitory had caught the striped bass for her.

"Betcha I could catch one of those at the pier," Joji bragged.

I knew for a fact that he couldn't possibly do that, but since I usually become my sweet and pleasant self around Christmastime, I left him alone.

Papa takes Joji fishing every once in a while, and

next to trying to learn how to drive, that is Joji's great passion. But it is certainly the last thing I want to do—go fishing, that is. I don't know why anybody wants to sit for hours on end, holding a pole with a string dangling from it. Besides, you've got to do horrible things before and after, like baiting the hook with a live, wriggling worm and then getting the slimy thrashing fish off the hook after you catch it.

"Ugh and double ugh," I say to Joji when he gets going about fishing. "You'll never get me to go with you."

And he answers, "Don't worry, Rinky-Dink, I ain't never gonna ask you to."

I was glad when Mr. Kinjo arrived with Mrs. S. and Boku and Mr. Sad Higa, because I'd had enough of fish talk.

I grabbed Boku by the arm as soon as he walked in.

"Hey, did you and your mama have that talk?" I asked.

"Yup," he said, nodding.

I was wondering if Mrs. S. had explained to him about his papa. I wondered if he knew his papa wasn't coming back. I was wondering how to ask him, when he told me himself.

"I gotta take care of my mama now, cuz Papa's gone," he said matter-of-factly.

I was surprised that Boku had turned out to be a pretty good kid, after all.

"Good for you," I said, giving him a friendly pat on

the back. Then, just before he pulled away from me, I added, "I think you're actually growing up, Boku."

That was certainly more than anybody had said to me lately.

Cal was having a friendly chat with Teru, and Papa was greeting everybody the way he does at church on Sundays. I was glad to see Auntie Hata and Mama bringing out all the food to the table, because I was absolutely famished.

Mama had brought one of my favorite dishes—*osushi,* which is flavored rice mixed with a lot of good stuff, like pieces of chicken and bamboo shoot and mushrooms and carrots, and sprinkled with shredded seaweed and strips of egg.

It was heaped on a big platter like a tiny mountain, topped with slivers of red ginger root, and I felt as though I could eat half the rice mountain all by myself.

It was a good thing Auntie Hata had made a lot of other things like sweet black beans and shredded long radish salad with sesame seeds. Also Mrs. S. had brought a big plate of fox ears—which is what I call fried beancurd cakes cut into triangles and stuffed with rice so they look like pointed fox ears.

It was like the feast Mama makes for New Year's, only today it was a wedding celebration and Christmas all mixed together.

"Now all you children, come get your food," Auntie Hata called out, "and sit anywhere you like on the floor."

Boku made a beeline for the table, took one look at

the striped bass, and growled, "Look out, ol' fish, I'm gonna eatcher eyeballs!"

"No, you're not," I heard Joji say to him, "I'm the one who's gonna do that. You can eat the tail."

Zenny and Abu were wrestling like two puppy dogs on the floor, ruining their clean shirts.

"Hey, cut that out!" I yelled at them. "Look what you're doing to your nice clothes."

But they just kept laughing and yelling and didn't pay the slightest attention to me.

Oh, gloom and doom, I thought miserably. Not only was I going to have to sit on the floor, I was going to be stuck with four noisy squabbling kids all through lunch. I was looking around for a cushion so I could at least be comfortable, when I heard Auntie Hata call me.

"Not you, Rinko," she said. "I borrowed enough chairs so you can sit at the table with the rest of us old folks."

"Oh, thank goodness!" I said, relieved.

It was almost as though Auntie Hata already knew something about me that I'd only find out later on. She'd just given me the first nice surprise of the day. The other one, which came later, I gave to myself.

XVII

ALL DURING LUNCH I KEPT WATCHING TERU FROM across the table and talked to her inside my head.

Golly, Teru, I said to myself, I guess I was a pretty lousy go-between, because the man I picked for you certainly didn't turn out to be much of a prince. And I couldn't save you from Mr. Kinjo after all. I guess I'm just a dumb kid, like you thought, and I guess Cal was right. I should have minded my own business.

I could have gone on for quite a while having this conversation inside my head, but suddenly I heard Papa stand up and clear his throat.

Oh-oh, I thought, he's going to give a speech.

I saw Joji grab Boku's hand and head for the door, because he knows about Papa's speeches and knows when to leave. Zenny and Abu were right behind them.

For just a second, I was tempted to go with them. I hate listening to long speeches, especially when they are in Japanese, and Papa can be very long-winded when he gets started. Sometimes I tell Papa he would make a good mayor, but he says he's not a politician and never wants to be one.

Cal noticed Joji's quick exit too. He leaned across the table and said to me, "Better escape now, too, while you can, Rink."

But I told him I was staying, because I knew I really didn't want to leave. I wanted to hear what Papa was going to say. I had a feeling he'd not only talk about the wedding, but he'd say something about the Big Trouble as well.

And I was right. That's exactly what Papa did, but for a minute, I thought he was trying to be a minister about to perform the wedding ceremony.

"We are gathered here today, my friends," he began, "to celebrate a truly happy and auspicious event."

"Don't make it too long, Papa," I muttered.

However, Papa ignored me and went on and on about how wonderful it was that Teru was reunited with her family, and how happy everyone was that she and Mr. Kinjo would be married soon. He smiled at them and congratulated them both. Then he turned serious. "But, of course," he said, "we are also concerned today about our friends Mrs. Sugino and Mr. Higa."

I saw them both lower their heads and look down at their laps. I knew Mrs. S. felt terrible because she hadn't been able to borrow anything close to the fifteen hundred dollars her husband had gambled away. And I thought probably Mr. Sad Higa was feeling pretty bad too. His whole body seemed to sag, as though he had a huge pack on his back and couldn't lift his head. I guess he was wishing he'd never been so dumb as to believe Mr. Sugino could double his life's savings for him.

Papa reached inside his jacket then and pulled out a small white envelope.

"It isn't as much as we'd hoped for," he said, "but please accept this as a gift from your friends."

Papa gave the envelope to Mr. Sad Higa, who looked as though he was about to cry.

"How can I accept this. . . ?" he began.

But before he could say anything more, Mr. Kinjo was on his feet.

"And please accept this as well," he said, giving Mr. Sad Higa a fatter envelope. "It is from Teru and myself. We could not be happy knowing two of our dear friends were enduring such pain, so we have decided—Teru and I—to postpone our wedding for a while."

A gasp went around the table, as though the wind had suddenly been knocked out of everybody.

"I had this set aside for our wedding and for starting our new home," he explained, "but I want you to have it, Higa. After all," he added, "what are friends for if not to help each other in time of trouble?"

He made it sound as though it was just the normal thing anybody would do, but I knew it was something pretty special.

Mr. Sad Higa wiped his face with a big white handkerchief and shook his head.

"Oh, no, Kinjo," he said. "This is asking too much of you. I cannot take it."

He tried to return the envelope, but Mr. Kinjo just pushed it back across the table. I don't know how long they would've gone on pushing that envelope back and forth if Papa hadn't said, "Take it, Mr. Higa. There is a time to give and a time to receive. We all want you to go home with your dream intact and Mrs. Sugino's honor restored."

"And you can rest assured," Mrs. S. added firmly, "that I shall repay Mr. Kinjo just as soon as I can work things out."

She stood up with her head held high and was the first to go shake Mr. Kinjo's hand and thank him.

Then something like bedlam broke out in the room. Everybody was telling Mr. Kinjo and Teru what good friends they were and saying how wonderful it was that everything had worked out. I guess maybe Mama had prayed real hard, and God had produced an honest-to-goodness miracle for her.

I looked at Teru, wondering if she was terribly disappointed about having her wedding postponed. Now she didn't know when she would get married, and maybe she wouldn't even get a gold ring when she did.

But the strange thing was, she didn't look sad or disappointed at all. She had this beautiful smile on her face, and her eyes were filled with tears. I saw her touch Mr. Kinjo's arm and say, "I know how long you have waited to have a wife, but I'm so glad we made this decision. You are a truly kind and generous person."

Mr. Kinjo smiled back at her. "I've waited many years, Teru," he said. "Another year or so won't matter now."

And when I saw the look Teru gave him, everything suddenly came clear. It was as though somebody had lifted me up so I could finally see over the big tall wall I'd built around myself.

I finally realized that Mr. Kinjo wasn't the wrong husband for Teru at all. He was exactly the *right* one. He'd been the right one all along. *He* was her happy ending, but I'd been too dumb to see that.

I also realized something else—that Teru wasn't just a pretty Japanese doll. She was a real woman, and she was strong, too, just like Mrs. Sugino and Auntie Hata and Mama. And her own dream was a lot better than the one I'd been trying to make for her. She'd made her own happiest ending without any help from me at all. I wondered how I could have made such a big mistake.

I went over to Auntie Hata and whispered in her ear. "You were right after all, Auntie Hata," I said. "It's going to be all right, just like you said."

"Of course," she said, nodding. "I knew it all along."

There was one more thing I had to do. I had to go talk to Mr. Kinjo at the other side of the table, and it was like walking uphill for six blocks to get there. There were a bunch of words I wanted to say to him, but I didn't know how to get started.

And that was when I surprised myself, because I suddenly said, "Golly, Mr. Kinjo, I sure was wrong. I'm sorry."

It was a great revelation to hear myself, because I didn't think I could ever say those words. But they had just popped out, and it hadn't been hard at all.

I didn't have to say anything more, because he knew exactly what I meant. I guess he'd never forgotten, anymore than I had, what I'd blurted out the first night I met him.

He just stood up and gave my hand a good, hard squeeze.

"Thank you, Rinko," he said. "You've made me very happy . . . very happy indeed, and I hope we will always be good friends."

I saw Teru watching us, and she nodded and smiled at me, as if to say she knew I understood at last and wasn't such a ninny after all.

Of course, Mama and Papa didn't know what was going on, because I never did tell them about trying to be a go-between. At least, I didn't think they knew. But I did see Mrs. S. give Mama a knowing glance. Maybe Mama did know everything after all, and had just left me alone to find things out for myself.

Anyway, I told Mrs. S. that I was glad her Big Problem had been solved, and she told me she felt wonderful.

Then she added, "Rinko, maybe you are the only one here today who knows just how happy and free I feel now."

I felt pretty good myself when I went back to my place at the table. I knew Cal was watching me, and when I looked up at him, he gave me a quick thumbs-up sign.

"Well, what d'you know, Rink," he said, with a friendly grin. "I do believe you're finally growing up."

But Cal really didn't have to tell me. I'd already discovered it for myself.

YOSHIKO UCHIDA has won many awards for her twenty-four books for young people and has also written many articles as well as a book for adults. Although her earlier books were about the folk tales and the children of Japan, her work now focuses on the Japanese American experience in the United States. She says of her recent work:

> "I hope to give young Asian Americans a sense of their past and to reinforce their pride and self-knowledge. At the same time, I want to dispel the stereotypic image still held by many non-Asians about the Japanese Americans and write about them as people. I hope to convey as well the strength of spirit and the sense of hope and purpose I have observed in many of the first-generation Japanese. Beyond that," she adds, "I write to celebrate our common humanity, for I feel the basic elements of humanity are present in all our strivings."

Yoshiko Uchida lives in Berkeley, California, the locale of her recent books.